PREMEDITAT

G000123893

SLOBODAN SELENIĆ was
published six novels and a number of plays, and was a member
of the Serbian Academy of Science and Arts and a professor at
the Conservatory of Dramatic Art in Belgrade. He is regarded
as one of the most important writers of his generation, and
was both winner of the prestigious NIN literary prize and
Belgrade's Poet Laureate. He died in 1995.

Slobodan Selenić

PREMEDITATED MURDER

*Translated from the Serbo-Croat
by Jelena Petrović*

THE HARVILL PRESS

LONDON

First published with the title *Ubistvo s Predumišljajem*, by
Prosveta, Belgrade, in 1993

First published in Great Britain in 1996 by
The Harvill Press
84 Thornhill Road
London N1 1RD

2 4 6 8 10 9 7 5 3 1

A CIP catalogue record for this book
is available from the British Library

Funded by
THE
ARTS
COUNCIL
OF ENGLAND

ISBN 1 86046 134 4

Designed and typeset in Monotype Minion and Walbaum
at Libanus Press, Marlborough, Wiltshire

Printed and bound in Great Britain by Butler & Tanner Ltd
at Selwood Printing, Burgess Hill

PREMEDITATED MURDER

The Love-Life of my Grandmother Jelena

ACKNOWLEDGMENT

See that? Acknowledgment. Like this is a real book or something!

Well, I *am* a writer – sort of. Or at least, I will be one shortly. I study drama – so you could say I'm almost there.

I'm not some smart-arse writer – I'll tell you that up front. I want to have my own style, know what I mean? I write like I talk and I talk as I damn please. That's basically my rule.

Of course, there's other things I do in life. I'm a photographer, for one. "Art" pictures. I do it for the dough, but somehow, it just doesn't do it for me.

This book, if I manage to get through with it, will not be written by me. What I mean is – I won't really "write it". I'll collect the pieces, I'll put them together. That is, if it doesn't bore me rigid in the process. Of course, I'll have to jazz it up a bit, because it's pretty sketchy. From the subtitle,which was my idea, like the title, you can tell it'll be juicy even though the book (whenever and however I happen to get it together) will be made up of bits and pieces. Jumbled bits and pieces at times. Obviously, it'll never be *Anna Karenina: The Sequel*, because what I found at the bottom of the canvas bag in Scumbag's closet is just a pile of patchy, accidental trinkets from my grandmother's life.

Then what's this acknowledgment thing? – you might ask. Well, I can't say I know, but it's chic to have one these days. Let me tell you – English and American University profs are mad about acknowledgments! They'd kill for their beloved acknowledgments! The fucking book is not complete until they've thanked half the human population of the US of A, plus their immediate and extended family. . . Some egghead lets a Cincinnati prof quote him, and the Yankee Doodle immediately pulls out the "I wish to acknowledge the courteous

3

permission. . ." bla bla bla. Or the lady next door says "Have a nice day" and he races to throw in a "My thanks are due to . . ." etc.

Well, since I too am an Author, I have to express my thanks. Who to? I haven't worked that one out yet. I won't sing the praises of Scumbag, of course, because she's a scummy. No thanks to Jovan either for his stuff (or "contribution", the more correct term), or to Jelena, for the letter. Why thank them? Let them thank *me* if by some divine intervention, their lives enter the Great Annals of Literature, to use a metaphorical expression. Speaking of which, a "Metaphor" is a little carriage-type thing that porters at Athens station use to transport people's luggage to and from the tracks. Saw it with my own eyes. Touched it. Spat on it too, when no one was watching.

Bla bla. Now, I'm metaphorically skipping Jovan and Jelena, but the person I *will* thank is this bloke Kojović, because I can tell from the outset he's going to be a big help. Helping the book "see the light of day", as the profs put it. The old man's a phenomenal talker, seriously. So we're going to use him for what he's worth. A talking book. In-fucking-credible! I set up my tape recorder, hit "on", and *voilà*, the book writes itself.

Secondly, the author wishes to thank her colleague Sreta Perić, alias Birdy, or more precisely – Birdy's dad, the benevolent history prof who promised me a glance or two at the police records for the year 1945. He's got loads of connections.

And lastly, I wish to thank Bonehead, mostly for just being around and putting up with me, for now. He wouldn't have, if he weren't such a bonehead.

Oh, I almost forgot: I "must express my endless gratitude" to that private publishing genius, my fat friend George Djurić, for not turning down, in these harsh times of war, a book about other people's grandmas.

"Not to worry, Bulika [that's what the genius calls me]. You just put it together, and leave the rest to me."

Okey-pokey, then. Here we go.

I

So here we are, in "The Blue Rider". Old Kojović and me. Round table, maroon tablecloth, ivory chairs. As if we were at the "Saint Mish".* In close-up. Major chaos around us. The place is swarming with "gentlemen strikers" from the Bermuda Triangle, which is what I call good old Belgrade University. The old man's looking at them sort of wistfully. I've noticed that look before . . . Fifty-year-olds tend to give us a mean kind of look. Really. Not all of them, of course. But eighty-year-olds go gooey at the sight of us. Why? I haven't the faintest. But it's weird.

Anyway, Kojović's about eighty himself, but he's slim and trim. You can tell by the cool moustache, the bow tie, the hair – the man hasn't given up. I mean, beige spats over a pair of perfectly lacquered black shoes? Christ.

Grandma Jelena used to call him "Old Fiacre",† and she was ten years younger than him. Well, *she* kicked the bucket over forty years ago, so work it out.

Anyway, I was worried his memory had retired, but surprise, surprise! Once Old Fiacre got going, there was no stopping him. You should have heard him tell his story. It's all like grammatically correct sentences, elegant phrasings, no trace of "like" and "you know". Makes sense. Ancient blokes like Kojović attended the Sremski Karlovci Gymnasium (is there *anyone* born in the BC era who *did not* attend that school?!) where rhetoric was a required subject. The man took

* The "Saint Mish" was a bar named after the Boulevard Saint Michel and thought to be very continental.
† Serbian original gives *fijker*, a carriage. An expression used in the 1940s for someone who is old-fashioned, whose dress and behaviour is dated and who is a little pretentious; someone who looks like a repainted old fiacre.

fucking exams in oratory skills! When he's quoting somebody, he transforms, you know – he sort of, *embodies* the new character. Stanislavski and shit. What's more, the old guy's having the time of his life. He obviously enjoys telling me all this. I'm enjoying it too. No rush to get to lectures – the whole damn university is on strike anyway. I sip my cappuccino. I listen. And here's what (edited by yours truly but nothing added):

ME:

So, major nightmare?

OLD FIACRE:

You mean . . .

ME:

Very tricky.

OLD FIACRE:

You seem to be asking if I was frightened. Well, it depends on one's viewpoint, Miss Jelena. After a long wait I was finally summoned into the office. The official simply said "Sit down" without so much as raising his eyes.

How shall I describe him . . . odd, isn't it, for a young person such as you to be gathering information on a long deceased grandmother. You are a curious young lady, Miss Jelena . . . Where was I . . . ? Oh yes, if my memory still serves me right, I remember him as a skinny man, small, rather ordinary, ungroomed, dressed in a uniform with a captain's insignia on the sleeve. He seemed young. They were all mere youngsters, his sort . . . Yet, I recall that he had a smoker's yellow complexion and conspicuous bags under his eyes.

"Kojović, Dr Branko Kojović?" he asked. "Are you a medical doctor?"

"No, actually. I am a doctor of philosophy."

My reply left no impression on him. If anything, he must have been amused, since in Communist jargon, one would call someone "philosopher" if one really wanted to insult them.

"Have you known Jovan and Jelena for long, Comrade Kojović?"

"From the cradle, so to speak. We used to live in neighbouring houses."

"So, you are friends then."

6

"I wouldn't say 'friends'. I am significantly older than the two of them. I was already a young man when they entered primary school."

"Did you see much of them during the German occupation?"

"Rarely. Both my house and the house of the Arandjelović family were confiscated in '41 by the Wehrmacht. Stavra Arandjelović and his children – Jovan and Jelena – moved to their other house in Krunska Street. I hadn't seen them for years, though I have been seeing Jelena more regularly since last December, when she came to work as a translator for Tanjug – our official press agency.

"Here I had to lie a little, Miss Jelena. What I mean is that even after we were forcibly removed from our old houses in Senjak, we were lucky to live in relative proximity to each other once again. The three of them were but a street away and we would run into each other daily. To be perfectly honest, I'd run into Mister Stavra more regularly, but I did see the two young Arandjelovićs as well. Naturally, I could not admit that to the official at the interrogation, as I was certain the compromising question would follow: "What was their political orientation during the occupation?" I avoided the question altogether by acting inept. I also emphasized that I saw Jelena frequently so as to avoid questions about Jovan. So I said: "I have been seeing Jelena daily, since she came to work for Tanjug."

"What about Jovan?"

"Hardly. Once or twice, maybe. Sometimes he waits for Jelena after work on the corner of Frankopanova Street . . ."

"What do you talk to him about?"

"The first time we ran into each other, we simply chatted about Senjak, our old neighbourhood. The second time, we merely exchanged greetings."

It happened just so, Miss Jelena. I don't recall him being particularly arrogant, merely disgusted at having to meddle with this. He seemed sick of it, sick of everything, I suppose. But tell me, am I being too broad?

ME:

Not at all.

OLD FIACRE:

Please, don't hesitate to say so. Just interrupt me if I wander off the track. Annoying folk seem to believe that all their experiences matter, even those from half a century ago. . . Half a century – that is how much time has passed since the interrogation. Somehow though, I remember everything. I remember, for example, that during the course of the interrogation, that dusty, unseemly little creature never once looked me in the eye. You see, insecure individuals tend to avoid people's eyes, and so do those who have something up their sleeve. I am not sure which of the two was the case with my interrogator. At any rate, he continued glaring at the papers before him and concluded:

"So, there's nothing you can tell us about Jovan Arandjelović?"

"Virtually nothing."

"What about Jelena?"

At this moment, old pruneface suddenly lost it. He obviously remembered something pretty bad, and it completely freaked him out. So he asks:

"Miss Jelena, do you wish to know absolutely everything about your late grandmother?"

The poor guy tensed up like a dead twig. He caught me in the middle of a sip there, so I couldn't answer immediately. I swallowed and said:

"Of course. Look, there's nothing to worry about, OK? I've never even seen Grandma Jelena! Go on, Mr Kojović, talk your heart out. Let's hear the Isadora Duncan saga."

This cooled him right off. He was concerned, but once he's been reassured, he'll return to his story – that sort of thing. What a honey.

OLD FIACRE:

Those were insensate times, Miss Jelena. Vulgar to the core, believe me. Now listen to what my interrogator asked me next:

"Does she sleep around?"

Though I knew that answers to the interrogator's questions needed to be well thought out, I had not prepared myself to expect such a level of vulgarity. Against my will, I exclaimed:

8

"Good heavens, of course not!"

The dusty captain instantly retaliated:

"And how would you know? Did you take notes by any chance?"

Dear God! Did I by any chance *take notes*?! Would you believe it? But – *qualis vir, talis oratio* – To each man his sermon.

Just think about it for a moment, Miss Jelena. Your grandmother Jelena was still very much a child in my mind, a younger sister almost, and whack! Does she sleep around?! Goodness gracious! It simply never entered my mind to pry into her love life! My acquaintance with her and her brother was of a completely different nature. I even remember changing Jelena's nappy once, when she soiled it in our back garden. I also remember that as children, neither Jovan nor Jelena could pronounce the letter "r". They used the letters "l" or "y" instead. "Blanko, Blanko, I'm scayed of that thing in the tlee!" Then one day, their first day of school as it happened, they both spontaneously mastered the elusive letter. Quite simultaneously and miraculously, they said "r". Earlier, I had promised them a dinar each if, in place of "dinal", they managed to pronounce the word correctly, and when they finally did, I gave it to them. For a bun at breaktime, or some such thing . . .

Where was I . . . ? Oh, of course: does Jelena Ljubisavljević-Arandjelović sleep around! Imagine! What sort of question is that, anyhow? Nonetheless, the vulgar candour of my dusty interrogator left a mark in my conscience, though I was not aware of it at the time. That night, I lay awake in my narrow bed in 27 Jevremova Street (having been thrown out of my flat in Hartvigova Street, that is where I had found temporary room, and that is where I am still living today – a half century later), and of all the captain's prying questions filling my head languidly and stubbornly like mud, or manure, forgive the expression, only the one regarding the suspected promiscuity of my little neighbour and friend Lena, alias Jelena, my beautiful colleague from the agency, kept me tossing and turning until dawn, when I finally drifted to sleep. Curious, isn't it? And now, fifty years later, you turn up and ask if I knew anything about your grandmother's love-life. May I ask why you wish to know about it, Miss Jelena?

I can tell the old man hasn't a clue about the existence of Jovan's manuscript and the rest of the papers from Scumbag's cupboard. Better not to mention anything.

ME:

I don't know. No reason. Actually, I know. You sort of hear everything about your grandma, but nothing about what she got up to in beddy-byes.

OLD FIACRE:

If Jelena, an unusually beautiful young woman, had any adventures of the romantic nature, I wouldn't be the one to know, Miss Jelena. Though, now that you ask, Krsman, Major Krsman Jakšić does come to mind. I recall you mentioning his name during our very first telephone conversation. Now, I must warn you, I don't know much, but I shall try to relate my memories in the most specific manner possible.

In the days following the interrogation, I tried summoning to mind as many detailed memories as possible of the encounters between Jelena and Krsman Jakšić. Naturally, whatever happened, or, more likely did not happen between the young victorious warrior and the beautiful Jelena could not be defined as "sleeping around". That term could only have been selected by a philistine Communist investigator in the moral and psychological morass that was Belgrade in the year 1945. However, I wouldn't be telling the whole truth if I failed to mention a sort of . . . tension . . . yes, tension, between the tall, dark-eyed and dark-skinned Krsman and that fragile, porcelain Aphrodite – your grandmother . . .

At this point, the old man stopped talking. Just like that. Retreated into his inner world, I suppose. He looks at me, then at the hordes of strikers all around us – the café is full to the brim, like a fucking bus right after the oil blockade – with this entranced look on his face. I'm checking the tape. I reckon, I'll just wait till he wakes up. No problemo.

OLD FIACRE:

As I look at you, dear young beauty . . .

Here, I realize that the old man's spiel is worth interrupting from time to time. To spare him the embarrassment of having to lie. Me? Beautiful? Amusing use of the word! A backside the size of Madagascar, a mop few have ventured to call hair, a few delight-inspiring blackheads . . . Fucking embarrassing! So I try turning the whole thing into a laugh:

ME:

So, do I look like the old granny in her youth?

Of course, I'm kidding in a major way, but the old man's dead serious:

OLD FIACRE:

No, I wouldn't say so. You are also beautiful but . . .

ME:

Me?! Beautiful?! You're kid . . .

OLD FIACRE:

. . . but you don't believe that you are. She was quite certain of her beauty. Also, you lack the kind of . . . let's see . . . what shall we call it . . . a very specific type of scorn for the male species, a kind of superiority I first noticed in Jelena and subsequently only in a few other women, all of them very beautiful . . . But that is not really what I was thinking about, Miss Jelena . . . that is not why I was looking at you. I look at you, Miss Jelena, and wonder: are you and your university colleagues, these young gentlemen students and revolutionaries, capable of seeing 1945 as it really was? I'm afraid that you are not. You see, the passage of time transforms an era into a legend. Ugly or beautiful; it matters not. I have been telling you everything as it truly happened, yet I still haven't told you what you really ought to know. Humans are not the only ones to age, you see; words age. They are born anew, identical in shape to their forebears, but changed somehow – mixed together with new implications, weighing sometimes more, sometimes less and bearing a different molecular structure.

For example, whatever the word Partisan may imply today – even at its most objective – Yugoslav Communists who fought against both the Royalists and the Axis powers, its meaning in 1945 was entirely different. Ah, the amount of self-adoration, hatred, the sheer volume of stories, memories, films and memoirs stored within that word in the last half-century! No, you simply cannot imagine what that word meant before your time. For those of us who *were* there, certain images will accompany us to the grave – shabby Partisans and Russian soldiers in delapidated trucks, lists of executed acquaintances published in the daily *Politika*, Tanjug, which was in the building of the pre-war agency Avala, Vladimir Dedijer, the Russian Colonel Morozov, even the petty Major Krsman. Your generation, on the other hand, will carry into the future an image of our time moulded by the knowledge and wisdom of your era. You will refer to 1945 using the same words, though words used differently back in 1945. For instance, I tried understanding the philosophies and actions of your colleagues – the new revolutionaries – by transporting them into the context of my era. But try as I may, I fail to see the connection between these revolutionaries and the revolutionaries at the University of Belgrade between the two wars. You simply don't resemble them, yet you are what they were in times now past – the revolutionaries from the University of Belgrade. The eyes of the old revolutionaries lit up with hunger, envy and cruelty . . . a kind of merciless justice.

ME:

And our eyes – what are they lit up with?

OLD FIACRE:

You are . . . clean, polished and frivolous. Of course, that's much more favourable than hunger and cruelty . . . (Kojović pauses for a bit again, then asks:) Am I talking nonsense?

ME:

Nope. I get what you're saying.

OLD FIACRE:

I was wondering if you could, to the best of your ability, picture how odd and unbridgeably different from each other these two characters appeared. Tanjug, winter of 1944: cosmopolitan and sophisticated Jelena, the princess from Senjak suddenly lost in an unbalanced world, her adored father wasting away in the Banjica jail and awaiting trial

12

before the "Court for the Trials of Crimes and Offences Against the Serbian National Honour", her brother only recently freed after two months of forced labour in the Bor mine, and Krsman Jakšić, OZNA major, which is to say, secret police agent, a former shepherd from some remote corner of the Kopaonik mountain. Those were truly insensate times, and that unholy alliance proves it.

So there we were, on the second floor of the Tanjug building. It was quite warm in our office . . . again here, even the simple word "warm" cannot mean to you what it meant to Belgraders that terrible winter. You see, fuel is one of the most reliable indicators not only of wealth but of the difference between life and death. To give you an example – you probably don't know the meaning of the word "frostbite", while most of those who survived the war had their feet covered with it in '44. Hence, it is warm in our office owing to a miracle, the miracle being several tons of unclaimed Silesian coal in the basement of the building. . . I promise that this is the last time I will pester you with the translation of a term from my era: the term "Silesian coal" doesn't have a close equivalent in the language of today. One might reach an approximation by cross-breeding the respective meanings of "platinum", "Deutschmark", "caviar" . . .

ME:

A lifetime supply of diesel at pennies a gallon?

OLD FIACRE:

Exactly – if there is no life without that diesel and it is glisteningly black, shiny, spotless like Silesian coal! As far as my tastes go, you know, Silesian coal is one of the three or four most beautiful things in the world. One almost feels sorry to burn it. It is so lovely, one would rather lick it! You see, the word "water" does not carry the same connotations for a bedouin as for a fisherman, though it represents the same thing. The word "snow" means endless masses of snow to an Eskimo. To an African, that word is something bizarre and improbable, like a celestial aberration. Anyway, in that warm room, you may interpret that as you wish, I sat at my desk, organizing the issues of international news which had been pouring in all morning long: French, English, American, German . . . the Soviets were late as usual . . . Normally, I would read the news and select the important items for Jelena to dictate to the secretary. But on that day, the secretary wasn't there. In fact, Jelena and I were the only employees present in the office. All the others were by the entrance, anticipating the arrival of Colonel Morozov, the Director General of the Soviet press agency TASS coming to visit our new head manager, Iva Vejvoda. "The Russian is coming! The TASS man is here!" . . . How can I even begin to describe the excitement and the fear, the anticipation . . .

ME:

Let's say – Extra-terrestrials have just invaded the planet. The boss of their news agency decides to drop round at today's Tanjug for a chat . . . Smart?

OLD FIACRE:

Very good, very good, Miss Jelena . . . Did you know that your grandmother was also in the habit of using that word – "smart"? Rather unusual for those times.

ME:

Spiritual telepathy. Zen Buddhism. Psychoanalysis. That's all I have to say.

OLD FIACRE:

Possible, very possible. "There are more things in Heaven and Earth, dear Horatio . . ."

ME:

So why didn't Grandma Jelena go out to greet the Soviet extra-terrestrial?

OLD FIACRE:

It wasn't exactly harmless not to join the collective on such occasions. On the contrary. So I said to her: "The directive specifies that I be the only one to stay on the news, Lena." She remained silent. "You have to go, Lena," I said; still not a word. I tried again: "You know how they look upon you . . . you don't even have to take it seriously – have a sense of humour about it; go, be amused by it all . . ." – that is when she replied, I recall very well:

"I would, Branko. I would for the sake of Stavra and Jovan, but I just can't do it yet."

That, Miss Jelena, is a sentence which floated through a river of hundreds of months and thousands of days, preserved in ice as it were, finally arriving here, at this table, finally confirming that it doesn't mean a thing to anyone in "The Blue Rider". Just as the avantgardist Kandinsky no longer does, am I right?

ME:

Well, it depends on where you stand. The Croatian author Krleza hated him. I, personally, like him.

OLD FIACRE:

I was introduced to him once.

ME:

To Krleza?

OLD FIACRE:

No, to Kandinsky. In Paris, in '36 or '37. He hardly spoke any French and my Russian was quite poor too. "Über das Geistige in der Kunst". Have you read it?

ME:

Nope. So what happens next? Did the beauty join the others in welcoming the extra-terrestrial beast?

OLD FIACRE:

Jelena? Not a chance. The beast came to see *her*. Not quite like that, but close enough. At some point, the extra-terrestrial, as you have so charmingly named the Soviet gentleman, took a guided tour of the agency. Eventually, they got to our office. Vejvoda, the head manager, opened the door, discreetly peeped in and moved aside to let his guest in. "Guest" if one is counting only Morozov; "guests", if one also counts their escort – Krsman Jakšić.

Kojović pauses – the advanced-level-rhetoric type of pause. He kind of lets that name resonate against the silence, if the idea of silence is conceivable in a room filled with a zillion apes conducting a political shouting match . . . anyway . . .

OLD FIACRE:

Comrade Vejvoda was . . .

ME:

Is that guy still alive?

OLD FIACRE:

No. He died a few months ago. Everyone has died. Sometimes it seems like I am the only one left. And they were all *so* alive! Take Vejvoda, for example. Veteran of the Spanish Civil War, member of the Supreme Command and of the Central Committee – decorations virtually coming out his ears. He was as excited as an adolescent rock fan about the arrival of this Morozov fellow – lively, energized, scurrying about, getting things done. He wanted the icy Tovarich to evaluate us positively. But you see, in spite of the Communist fashion and the vulgar customs of these new world rulers, Vejvoda, a Communist himself, was a pleasant and amiable man. He used the very words which caused panic and suspicion among the Communists – words such as "Good day" and "Excuse me". He even introduced us to the Russian ceremoniously, reverentially. And here, *here* precisely begins the story of the heroism, or madness, of your grandmother, Jelena Ljubisavljević-Arandjelović.

ME:

All right. Let's hear it.

OLD FIACRE:

Let me tell you one thing before I begin. You see, I am not a hero. I have always been a little resentful of heroism. A hero, in my mind, can only be a profiteer, or someone who overestimates the goal in the name of which he exposes himself to danger. I always do only what is expected of me, never more, sometimes even less. Hence, when introduced to a Soviet colonel, I force my lips into an apish smile satiated with optimism and hope for the socialist future – an emblem, I should add, of Bolshevik spirituality – all the while shaking his hand long and hard, as I saw it done in some Soviet documentary clip of Party clansmen shaking hands with the socialist builders of yet another "Economic Giant".

So that is what I did. Now wait till you hear what your grandmother did.

After a polite though restrained nod of the head in acknowledg-

16

ment of the important guest, Miss Ljubisavljević-Arandjelović calmly continued typing!

Vejvoda's face turned blood red with embarrassment and uncertainty over what to do next, while Morozov, cooler by several degrees, registered the event as well as its participants in his fat police file. Jelena, I had noticed, was fully engrossed in her work at that moment, purposely beautiful (real beauties can do that, I promise you. I know what I'm talking about), angelic, simultaneously virginally pure and firm, square-shouldered like a diamond. A true Antigone! I admired her beauty at that moment, but I did not admire her heroism. Although, perhaps that wasn't heroism on her part, but a cunning ability to outfox anyone. I will explain quickly. You see, I have yet to meet the person who would dare make such a political faux pas and manage to evade its consequences. Anyone would make concessions even of the smallest kind – anyone would, for example, stop typing for a moment and smile.

Not Jelena! I don't know how she managed it, but she did. On the occasion I am describing, everybody reckoned that an even greater scandal would ensue if this cock-up by the black sheep in the family were called to attention. It seemed most appropriate to simply ignore it and refrain from interpreting the behaviour of this black sheep. The *dangerous* behaviour, I should add. Indeed, Jelena was always capable of defending her right to uniqueness amidst their unfledged and hot-headed philosophy of sameness.

In those first months following the liberation from the Nazis, any deviation from Communist beliefs, the parameters of fashion, codes of behaviour and expression was downright dangerous. Peasant dialects, the sleepless tired look of the socialist activist, a copy of *The History of the All-Union Communist Party (Bolsheviks)* under one arm, coarse Partisan uniforms and the obligatory red star on the Titovka, the hat named after Marshal Tito – all that was part of the "look", the bolshevik "allure" adopted obediently and more or less adeptly by what remained of Belgrade's bourgeoisie.

Not by the black sheep Jelena! Deliberately and conspicuously different, your grandmother managed with some special knack to present her uniqueness in dress, language and humour as a quirky aspect of her character rather than a political statement. That was her secret. For example, since she (like all others) was prohibited from addressing people with "Mister" and "Madam" and could not bring herself to utter the formulaic "Comrade" she came up with a great ruse: To the men, she would say "Tovarich" and to the women, the Macedonian "Drugarkata"! Naturally, they suspected it was some kind of bourgeois mockery, but how could they criticize her for using the languages of our two great Slavic-Bolshevik-Proletarian brother nations?

In her style of dress, she was just as outrageous! Ah, dear Miss Jelena, I get shivers remembering it. You simply cannot imagine what it meant to wear an astrakhan fur coat with matching muff, a pleated skirt, silk stockings, high-heeled shoes and veiled hat among the staunch comrades of our agency. I cannot even begin to guess where she managed to find such a wardrobe in impoverished Belgrade, where everyone had long ago exchanged all their valuables for flour and oil. One day, she came into the office wearing elbow-length black fishnet gloves! Milesa Vučelić, one of our superiors, was appalled:

"What is that junk on your arms, you little vixen?" she asked furiously.

"Gloves," Jelena replied, quite unexcitedly.

"I can see that. Why in hell are they full of holes?"

"These are the only ones I have." And as if that were not enough, she added in absolute seriousness: "These are hard times, Drugarkata Milesa. You know how it is – all to the front, all for the front."

And that passed too. She got away with it once again. Milesa, as well as several other bigoted, or "aware" Comrades, as they were called at the time at the agency, tried to initiate an investigation into the matter of Jelena's "Anti-Socialist" behaviour, but they remained unsuccessful.

ME:

How did Krsman look upon Jelena's faux pas towards the extra-terrestrial Big Brother?

OLD FIACRE:

I don't know. I didn't pay any attention to him at that moment. I was observing Morozov and Vejvoda. Much later, Krsman told us what exactly happened as the delegation left our room. The Russian stopped walking, assembled his thoughts for a moment and asked: "Eta Devushka, krasavitsa – ona bespartiinaia?" (That girl, the pretty one, isn't she in the Party?)

Vejvoda shrugged his shoulders and shook his head apologetically:

"Shortage of personnel, I'm afraid. We need her, comrade Morozov. She is fluent in French and English."

"Ia ponimaiu, Ia ponimaiu" (I understand, I understand), Morozov replied. As to what he really thought and wrote down in his report, God only knows. I remember asking Krsman:

"Did Comrade Morozov really say 'krasavitsa'?"

"Yeah. But he didn't really mean it, y'know? Was like, what d'you call it – irony? Yeah, irony."

ME:

So, from this time on, Krsman sort of became a regular at your office?

OLD FIACRE:

Yes. He had no business whatsoever on the second floor, in our office. His job was to accompany the head honchos around the building; he was a major, a big fish. Still, there he was – in the beginning, he came around every two to three days and later on, several times each day. Storming into the room, he would shout a proletarian slogan of one type or another, always enthusiastically, but from the vertical distance of his military rank:

"Full steam ahead, Comrades! That's right, keep it up! Nobody rests while we build a new country!"

"What's new today, Comrade journalists? Berlin fall yet?"

Krsman was a handsome man, very handsome. One might have mistaken him for a gipsy, or a subcontinental Indian, but a very handsome gipsy, a handsome Indian film star. His eyes were dark, incredibly dark and shiny. He was tall, thin. A robust, strong animal, one could say, Miss Jelena. One had the impression that there was something cat-like about him, that something very agile and strong lay hidden beneath his major's uniform of real English wool. Now, was it English? In '44? Yes, I think it was. The "diplomatic warehouses" did not exist yet, but the Communists were already procuring for themselves things we could not even dream about. English or domestic wool, all the same. The man had enough vigour for the population of a small village! He smelled of the leather of his belt, his straps and his pistol case.

As for his Serbian, it was appalling. He had lived in a mountain hamlet as a child; at the age of fifteen, he moved to Kraljevo, where he worked as a baker's apprentice. His accent was very strong, as you can imagine. He wasn't ashamed of it, though. I would even say that he purposely flaunted it, either because he took pride in the nobility of his plebeian origins, or to express his resentment for Belgrade's bourgeoisie.

"You think I can't talk like you talk? 'Course I can. I talk my way cuz it's better," he would say with a broad grin on his face, brimming with untenable joie de vivre, overjoyed at having survived the war, convinced that nobody could do him any harm. Nobody except the "class enemy", of course, but that was an abstract term for them, not a collection of human beings.

All of his expressions were peasant sayings, and they were often quite vivid: "All the things a livin' man needs" was one. He would say that often, using it mostly as an interjection. Or once, for example, commenting on one of Churchill's long (in his opinion overly long) speeches: "He got small brains in that big bald head so they just keep on spinnin'." Can you believe it, Miss Jelena? Saying such a thing about Churchill?! The Communists are blasphemers and desecrators. And if someone asked him where he was going, he would reply with a mixture of countryboy mischief and arm-of-the-law mysteriousness: "To buy myself a lollipop".

We all knew that Major Krsman made his frequent excursions to the second floor for Jelena. He never even tried to conceal it, though he always had an excuse. Once it was coffee – he brought us all some, which was an extraordinary luxury in those days. Another time, he brought chocolate. Real chocolate! Nestlé chocolate – another rarity which nobody had even *seen* since before the war. When he wasn't treating us to food, he would come in pretending to be interested in the latest news. He would ask me to read to him from the print-outs, but he wouldn't even listen – he was too busy looking for the right moment to approach Jelena. And everyone, absolutely everyone knew it.

ME:

Except Jelena.

OLD FIACRE:

Precisely! Lena did not have the faintest shade of an idea! Jelena was the detached Olympian, my dear young friend. She didn't dislike him, find him repulsive or anything of the sort. Of course, one couldn't say she was pleasant, but she wasn't unpleasant either. Jelena was simply polite, absentminded and terribly distant. She would talk to him sometimes, answer his questions politely, briefly, concisely, but with the dreamy distance of some harmless lunatic. I don't know how else to describe it, Miss Jelena. She remained simply untouchable.

ME:

Sort of like bullfighting.

OLD FIACRE:

I'm not sure that I understand.

ME:

I mean – was she playing hard to get or did she just not give three shits about the bloke?

OLD FIACRE:

My dear Miss Jelena, if I knew the answer to that question, my knowledge of your grandmother's personality would be far more conclusive than it is. You see, Krsman was famous for his love conquests. He broke fragile – are they not, Miss Jelena? – female hearts frequently and mercilessly. He was the prototypical young hero. Handsome. Strong. Charming and ruthless. Romantic. Covered with blood, tired of killing. And barely twenty-six years old! It was rumoured that he had killed a thousand men and seduced as many women. The figure needn't have been correct but it made him even more desirable. He had a massive female following at Tanjug as well. Thus you can imagine how Jelena's icy aloofness bordering on contemptuous indifference drove the large corps of Tanjug's females to a frenzy.

To be honest, Jelena was despised by the women even before Krsman came to Tanjug. They despised her because there are certain kinds of women other women simply do not like. There *are* such women, believe me. They go through life adored at every step by men, all the while never succeeding in developing a single female friendship. Not even a mere acquaintance. Well, Jelena was one such woman. She had absolutely no female friends, not one. Her one and only friend was her brother Jovan, who, as you know, was not her real brother (indeed, her life was unique in every respect, including family), nor was he close or distant kin, though they were virtual twins. Hence, when one adds to Jelena's congenital inability to form female friendships the Partisan prince's ardent interest in her, and tops it all with Jelena's dreamy unawareness of the prince's existence, you can imagine, my dear young friend, what sort of restrained and for that, all the more destructive fury was accumulating in the female hearts of Tanjug's defeated beauties . . .

ME:

And Krsman? Was he pissed off by his lack of success?

OLD FIACRE:

My impression was that Krsman went through a veritable sort of lover's Golgotha; experiencing humiliation at each stop along the Via Dolorosa! It was like in the movies, truly. It amused me greatly to watch his speedy transitions from one emotional state to another. In the beginning – cynicism: his sparkly eyes are posing the conceited question "Why don't you surrender, young lady? Can't you see I'm irresistible?"

ME:

And Jelena?

OLD FIACRE:

Jelena doesn't hear the question, of course. This stage is then followed by true surprise: "Hmm . . . Does this young lady really not care for me? Why?!"

That last question was probably accentuated by another, repressed question: "Is it because I'm a baker, because I'm a peasant?"

ME (retardedly):

And Jelena?

OLD FIACRE:

Once again, Jelena is innocently looking through Krsman, entirely unaffected.

At stage three, Krsman loses his temper. He becomes vulgar and screams across the room:

"Blimey, some women are bitches, real bitches. My buddy Zvonko, know what he told me? He told me those spoilt bourgeois girls are good for nothin', he said. All they're good for is giving you VD. And you, Milesa, better be more careful what kinda scum you hire!"

At this point, Jelena turns to me and tells me loudly enough so that everyone could hear her: "Branko, be kind enough – open a few windows. It's rather stuffy in here." Then she gets up, walks across the room towards the door, slowing down her step as she passes Krsman, staring straight into his eyes with the sweetest smile on her lips.

In January of 1945, Krsman started showing signs of serious obsession. At the office New Year's Eve dinner party, he seduced Milesa. Proud of her success and full of resentment for Jelena, Milesa began dropping by our office on a regular basis, showing herself off like an exotic bird. She would even refer to Krsman as "my man", I remember that detail quite well. Once again, everyone knew, except the dreamily absent, harmless eccentric Jelena.

Towards the end of January, Krsman arrived at the thirteenth and penultimate station of his love journey: bewilderment. Jelena's Greenlandian indifference made his strategic affair with Milesa appear ridiculous. Once, when he heard her refer to him as "my man", he slapped Milesa, before everybody.

We were all startled.

All, except Jelena. She didn't even notice anything unusual in the room . . . so, that's how it went – a veritable sado-masochistic cartoon in fourteen episodes.

ME:

You didn't mention anything about fourteen. What happened in episode fourteen?

OLD FIACRE:

The tamer of the beast triumphs! Following a two-week absence, a broken, insecure, diminutive and foolish man who even spoke with a city accent, came back to our office.

ME:

And Jelena?

OLD FIACRE:

Distant as America, my dear friend.

ME:

So, you could call it bullfighting, then. Castration or – "the process of turning the Communist stallion into a mere Serbian ox".

OLD FIACRE:

It's very possible. However, this is not where the story ends. In fact, its most curious episode has not even begun yet. Shortly afterwards, towards the end of January, I believe, Jelena did something incredible, something utterly incongruous with her pride, her comportment, her imperial superiority.

ME:

Bingo! Let me guess: horizontal activities?

OLD FIACRE:

No, good heavens, no! You're going a little too far, Miss Jelena. Besides, how could I testify to that? Nothing of the horizontal sort took place, as far as I know. But as the international law dictionary states so eloquently – Jelena *recognized* Krsman Jakšić.

ME:

Here comes the coffee at last.

OLD FIACRE:

Here's how it all happened. You see, we were alone in the room, Jelena and I, when the handsome major came in and embarked upon a circumambulatory, nervous, tentative discussion about the political situation or some such thing. Nothing unusual, I would have thought. However, to my complete astonishment, the dreamily absent Jelena suddenly interrupted our conversation with the most unexpected question. It was as if a spirit had spoken, as if she had finally ventured back to our world from a strange, cloud-borne realm:

"Major Jakšić," – she did not say Comrade, I remember very well, and she didn't use her mocking "Tovarich" either – "could you please find out where my stepfather Stavra Arandjelović has been detained and when he will face trial?"

I was so surprised by Jelena's question, dear Miss Jelena, that yet again I had no time to be surprised, this time at the fact that Krsman replied instantly, as if he had prepared his answer long ago and rehearsed it ad infinitum in his mind.

"He's in the Banjica jail. When his trial's gonna be, that I don't know. When they finish the investigation, I s'pose."

Here comes Bonehead. He stands by the table, leaning on his crutches.

"Why don't you sit down?" I ask.

Bonehead looks around, hopelessly. The strikers, or "revolution-aries", as Kojović would put it, have invaded "The Blue Rider" and have now taken over the premises down to the last sliver. No trace of a chair.

"Go and mingle with those crutches of yours. Maybe someone will honour you with a chair," I advise.

While Bonehead's mingling, Kojović asks:

"And the young gentleman is . . . ?"

"I found Bonehead on a park bench. About a month ago. He came from Moslavina."

"Moslavina? Where exactly is that?"

"Nobody knows. Personally, I think the place doesn't exist. Bonehead made it up so he could say he has a hometown."

"Was he injured in this war?"

"Yeah. He's one of those wild beasts who eat little kids. Catholic, Croatian kids, if you know what I mean. I still find him sweet, though."

Bonehead comes back with a chair and sits down between me and the old man. Props his crutches against the table. Bye-bye conversation, for now. So I grab his chin and I say to Kojović:

"He's a real sweetie, isn't he? Isn't he gorgeous?"

The old man's uncomfortable, so he blurts out in Latin:

"Uh . . . Oh, certainly, certainly! *Iuventus ventus.*"

"Pretty as a calf!" I say. Bonehead smiles innocently, good-natured as ever.

Kojović, of course, understands the virtue of social graces:

"Allow me to introduce myself, young man. My name is Branko Kojović."

Bonehead shakes Kojović's hand but doesn't say his name. I must've confused him. He doesn't mind me teasing him, but he never seems to get used to it. I issue a warning:

"Tell the gentleman your name."

"Bogdan Bilogorac."

"Are you a student, Mr Bilogorac?"

"I was a student, in Osijek. Now I'm a soldier. Artillery."

Apropos of which, I tell Kojović:

"Mister Kojović, let me tell you what I conveyed to this creature here: if he ever goes to fight for that Serbian cause thing again" (and here I was tempted to say "their fucking Serbian cause from hell and their medieval fucking battles", but swearing just doesn't go with beige spats, so I refrained),"he can kiss me goodbye. He can go off and die a mythic death in the battle for the famous Moslavina fortress. No skin off my nose."

"Come on, Jela, don't talk like that," Bonehead says semi-reproach-fully, not at the death bit, that's for sure (he'd put his life on the line any day of the week) but because of my anti-Serbian commentary.

But I could smell the end of this rap session, so we got our arses in gear. It was late anyway, and recently I've had to take Bonehead for checkups and bandage changes in the fucking dead of night.

As soon as we got off our arses, a charming company of revolution-aries sprang towards us and grabbed our chairs. Nearly knocked down the old guy and my little crippled friend. But we survived. All's well that ends well, bla bla.

II

Actually, this book was Bonehead's idea. Well, not entirely. Even when I first read Grandpa/Uncle Jovan's manuscript, which was five years ago, I thought it needed to be put to some kind of use. It was just sitting there, rotting away along with some other papers. Real literature and all that. A real live finished novel waiting around at the bottom of some bag.

And then of course, the stuff wasn't about just anybody – it concerned the lives of my recent ancestors – Grandmother Jelena and Grandfather/Uncle Jovan.

So anyway, I had no clue what Jovan's manuscript really was and how it ended up in the bag in the first place. I didn't know if Jovan would've wanted me to publish his whatever-it-is. I also didn't know what my grandmother would say if I published her letter, which she apparently never posted. As for what Scumbag would say, I didn't give a toss. I've been hating her pretty intensely since around that time, five years ago.

But that's not the point, now. I dumped Jovan's manuscript (single spaced type. The paper yellow around the edges. Sheets held together with a sewing pin. No pencil corrections anywhere. A longer, narrower format than usual) back into the bag. Did nothing about it. As usual. Well, later on, it started to bug me. I'd been itching to become a writer and also, I'd always wanted to learn more about the whats whens and wheres of Scumbag's mother – my grandmother – in those primeval days, around Anno Domini 1945. I knew bits of the story, of course, but there was lots I didn't know. That's what I wanted to find out. I was even more curious about the stuff I already knew – a "real novel"!

27

Before I go on, I have to admit one thing: there's plenty of gaps in the damn thing. But then again, who says you got to spell everything out for the reader? Let him be a little inventive! Gaps or no gaps, it's a fucking volume. Greek drama. Action-packed, I-laughed-I-cried material. How to become a writer in five easy lessons . . .

Anyway, the stuff grabbed me, but it didn't grab me enough. So I gave up on it, and eventually, I forgot. Meanwhile, the family saga sits and rots.

Then one day, I met Bonehead. Maybe this isn't important, but I'll tell you anyway. So, as I said, one day, I picked up Bonehead in a park and brought him home. I could tell immediately – he was an original, a genuine Bonehead: came from some dead-end village called Moslavina, attended a classical gymnasium, currently studies Geodesy part-time and fights for the liberation of "old Serbian territories". I mean, you won't see this kind of phenomenon in many places. Weak, sick, wounded, quiet as a mouse, pretty as a calf, wouldn't bother you if he was trapped under a ten-ton truck. So, the Florence Nightingale that I am, I thought I'd get him to relax and feel at home by reading him some non-fiction:

"Want to read this text I got?"

He nods yes. Doesn't even ask what kind of text. So I get the bag. I read it to him, the beginning of Jovan's whatever the fuck it is – confession, shall we say. Six pages, single spaced, so about twelve:

JOVAN:

The argument over Stavra's biography began as soon as Lena told me she would write it. It was a Saturday at the beginning of January. Or was it the end of January? Regardless, it was most certainly a Saturday. "For God's sake, Jelena, why?" I asked.

All day long, while she typed, I invoked new reasons as to why her attempt at paying court to the Communist barbarian was humiliating and pointless: Krsman Jakšić! That mountain bandit! He's not capable of helping anyone, much less you! He's a peasant, a policeman, a thug! And why do you think Stavra deserves that biography? Do you think that those criminals will release him because of something we've scribbled on a piece of paper?! Those barbarians don't even know all the letters of the alphabet!

She didn't respond to my nagging until evening, when like a bolt from the blue, she said:

"He isn't quite ordinary."

This is how it all began.

"Who?" I asked.

"The Communist barbarian."

I was startled. Speechless. Before I came to my senses, she added: "He is beginning to manifest certain human qualities."

"Krsman?" I asked.

"Yes."

"Human?"

"Well, let's say, human*like*, parahuman."

I did not dare continue this conversation. I am writing this in the hope that I will comprehend the words I suppressed that day. Suppressed? Not quite. Jelena, braver than me, had initiated this conversation, but I allowed it to disintegrate quickly into a bitter argument over trivia. Any topic was good enough, providing it led us as far away as possible from the monster in our cellar, which, I was certain, would be under surveillance as long as we were waging our war with words that didn't matter. We argued until dawn about everything from soup to nuts. We were both extremely drunk, yet neither Jelena nor I said what I will now attempt to write down. Surely I must. I want to see how the unspoken reality looks when it is transformed into words.

I had the impression that at the end, intoxicated and exhausted by the dispute, Jelena silently complied with my plea not to write Stavra's biography. Before falling asleep, feeling garrulous from the sickly-sweet eggnog (a truly disgusting drink) drawn from our last war reserves, I thought to myself victoriously – she gave in! A good sign. Maybe not everything is as black as I thought it was.

I know Jelena. I know her better than anyone else in this world. Sure enough, the following day began as all other days in our little household would begin ever since the liberators occupied Belgrade. I said:

"Pigs!" Quietly. I absentmindedly rumpled the front page of the *Borba* with both hands. Staring at the keys of the typewriter, Jelena paused and said:

"So why do you read it then?" – her question always sounded like a phonographically metallic echo of the word "pigs".

We had been exchanging the same words followed by the same gestures every day since November of '44, when the dailies had begun publishing their lists of executed war criminals and German collaborators. But that January morning in '45, as I threw the crumpled newspaper ball aiming for the dustbin by Jelena's desk, I became aware for the very first time of the ritualistic nature of this regular morning exchange. I realized that Jelena's question was fitting. Why do I keep doing it? Why do I keep reading e-ve-ry morning about the military tribunal's "effort to cleanse society of fascist heritage"? Do I hope to find information on Stavra? Or am I really doing it for the reward of disgustedly uttering the therapeutic word "pigs" and always hearing the same reply while aiming for the dustbin: "So why do you read it then?"

Having become so suddenly aware of the incantatory nature of my curse and of Jelena's reproachful reply, I noticed that the daily ritual had gradually lost most of the momentum of our impotent wrath. Three or four months earlier, when I was deeply shaken and still not numbed by the biblical dissolution of Jelena's and my world, the pronouncement "Pigs!" sounded like a cry of war: before leaving for my shift in the forced labour mine of Bor, I would scream, furiously crumpling the front page, vengefully shredding it and usually missing the dustbin by Jelena's work desk in the mad effort to free my hands from that piece of printed filth. On that Saturday morning, however, I realized for the first time that my pronouncement sounded tired and that I was crumpling the two pages slowly, thoughtfully, trying, as a child might, to make a solid ball with which to score my goal.

Startled, I also remembered that several days earlier, I stood and watched impassively as the executors from the district court came in and confiscated Stavra's suits, shirts, shoes, pyjamas – as if his factories, houses and bank accounts had not been enough.

*   *   *

Bonehead and I later found this document in Stavra Arandjelović's file in the Archives of the Republic of Serbia:

Number 4658/45, 23.01.45.

IN THE NAME OF THE PEOPLE

The People's Court of the Seventh District of the City of Belgrade presided over by judge Milenko J. Polovina, jurors Jovanić Mirko and Stefanović Dušan and court clerk Mira Ranić on the subject of the third party claim of Jovan Arandjelović, residing at 24 Krunska Street, as represented by public defender Blažo Radović, petitioning for the right to movable property confiscated and inventoried on December 27th 1944 from Stavra Arandjelović, who was prosecuted according to article c.#246/45 on December 14th 1944 for criminal offence against the Serbian National Honour. In the presence of the representatives of the People's Administration of Public Property, this court has reached the following

VERDICT:

1) The court recognizes the right to moveable property for Jovan Arandjelović and Jelena Ljubisavljević-Arandjelović for the items located in 24 Krunska Street. The items are as follows:

2 beds, including linen items (mattresses, pillows, sheets and blankets), 1 armchair, 2 chairs, 1 small and 1 larger rug, 2 night tables, 3 cupboards, 3 large closets, 1 sofa, 1 small table, 1 light fixture, 2 sets of curtains.

2) Under Article 6 regarding the confiscation of property from Stavra Arandjelović, the following items remain exempt as they are understood to be indispensable to the subject: 2 men's shirts, 2 pairs of underwear, 2 pairs of socks, 1 suit, 1 pair of trousers, 1 hat, 1 pair of shoes, 1 pair of boots, 1 pair of galoshes, 2 handkerchiefs, 1 pair of pyjamas, 1 winter coat, 1 leather bag, 1 raincoat.

The remainder of the inventoried items are: 19 men's shirts, 6 suits, 14 pairs of socks, 4 hats, 6 pairs of shoes, 8 pairs of pyjamas, 14 pairs of underwear, 4 bathrobes, 2 pairs of galoshes, 26 handkerchiefs, 2 winter coats, 3 jackets, in addition to the previously evacuated furniture and other moveable property taken out of the 24 Krunska Street residence on January 21 1945. All of the above mentioned items are hereby declared state property.

3) This verdict goes into effect on this day, the 23rd of January 1945.

This is followed by the prosecution's closing argument but it's as boring as hell. In addition, the document is transcribed by hand and partially illegible. Mainly, the witnesses are describing Stavra as a slave driver. We'll find room for that elsewhere. At the end, it says:

The representative of the People's Administration of Public Property has left the evaluation of the validity of witness testimonies up to the court and ultimately, the decision itself. It is in light of that information that the verdict has been reached.
The Seventh District Court of the City of Belgrade

23.01.1945
Judge
Milenko Polovina

At first, Bonehead was against my sticking the verdict in here, because we didn't know it existed the first time I read him Jovan's manuscript. But I convinced him that it looks just brilliant here.* And now, we return to Jovan's manuscript:

I was taken aback by the sudden, truthful echo of the word "numbed".

"We only have the impression that we are not changing," I said, saddened by the discovery that our hatred was frail before the hordes of vileness advancing upon us from every direction. Krsman's suggestion that Jelena or I write Stavra's biography was certainly one of them.

---

* This is what you call "methodology", man! Here we are, arranging stuff from the bag, but we're also describing how we're doing it. Bonehead said it right: "It's a book about how we made the book."

"You think we're changing?" she asked, without interrupting her typing.

"I think that humans, that even we, Jelena, get accustomed to the worst with deplorable ease," I replied, certain she would understand that I was referring to her decision to collaborate with Krsman. I did not expect that she would continue to race with such determination wherever she intended to arrive at any price.

"I'm finishing the biography," she said.

Those words explained everything.

The world was slipping away from under my feet. I felt it with my big toes. I needed to be sure that it was still there. Wrong evaluation. I had incorrectly assessed the end of our drunken brawl. I, who know Jelena better than anyone else in this world. She had not given in.

When I gathered my wits, I realized that I could not afford to surrender either. Having expended my quarrelling energy, I decided to try crushing Jelena's persistence in a pacificatory manner. I hastily formulated the sentence:

"The Arc of two righteous persons glides upon the deluge of crudity."

I'm turning into a toy-poodle. I'm standing on my hind legs, licking her hand and squealing affectionately.

This carefully constructed and moderately pompous sentence was a clear introduction to the "Game of Literary Deceits" which Jelena and I loved playing. We had invented the game in our very early youth. For a long time, we had needed the presence of a third party, or third parties, in order to play the game. Its objective was to compose a sentence whose literary value would seem unsurpassably elegant and profound to Miss Melanija, Mr Stojic – our professor of algebra and geometry – friends we wished to fool, or indeed to anybody constituting the "third party", while us two, arrogantly amused by our shrewd trick, were the only ones aware of its badly concealed frivolity and kitschy vulgarity.

As we matured, the game did not change in essence, though it grew more sophisticated. For years now, we had had no need for the presence of "others". We would imagine "others". We laughed at them in their absence. It sufficed to simply picture the outwitted party, which represented the whole world to us at that moment.

I did not know how much Jelena would appreciate the Arc gliding upon the deluge of crudity. I knew that the sentence did not belong among the jewels of our ingenuity. It was not baroque enough, it wasn't stupid enough underneath its frills and furbelows and even the imaginary others could penetrate to the heart of its banality. At that moment, however, I wasn't capable of constructing a better trap-phrase. Thus, I uttered it as a symbol of goodwill, an end to all animosities and an invitation to reconciliation.

Naturally, Jelena had understood everything. She smiled. Reservedly. She did not stop typing. She did not raise her beautiful head from the keys, she did not move the disobedient lock of hair from her exquisitely white face with a nonchalant brush of the hand (a gesture I love so). Cautiously, and rightfully so, she understood that I was not initiating the game but rather continuing my struggle against the writing of Stavra's biography through other means. We still called it that. We still avoided using real words, although we knew that we were roaming the dangerous vicinity of the entrance to our bolted cellar. I concluded that Jelena knew I wished to dissuade her from her embarrassing and pointless intentions by means of kind supplication after my angry cursing had proven futile. But to no avail.

Jelena finished the "Biography" towards evening on that same day.

"Would you like to read it?" she asked, looking straight into my eyes.

I lowered my gaze. I dared not read in her eyes the answers to those questions which I was forced to, at least at that instant, hide from myself; to save them for this wretched treatise.

"No," I replied.

The trouble was: while I knew what was passing through Jelena's capricious and recalcitrant head at every moment, I also knew that Jelena knew it. She knew that I was reading her thoughts, and she knew simultaneously what thoughts were buzzing through my mind. It had always been so. As far as I was concerned, at least. It seems to me that I had begun noticing Jelena's feelings even before I became aware of my own; I had spoken my first words through her thoughts, not mine, and I dare even suspect that I had become aware of Jelena's existence before I had realized my own.

I know, I am certain, though I do not know the origin of this certainty, that my first memory of Jelena is a murky notion of pink. An awareness of a pink rattle, a pink potty or a pink hat on the head of my other baby half. The notion of pink is a sensation recorded inside me before my soft infant brain started to distinguish objects and before – I am convinced of it – I could separate myself from my surroundings.

Pink. The primordial pink before which nothing was. Void. The cosmic void of infinity. Infinity – a term the human brain is incapable of subordinating.

I cannot describe pink – the pink of the primordial thought, the pink of Jelena's existence. I cannot say when the stimulus began inhabiting my baby brain. Was it when I was ten months old, one year old, maybe later? However, I am positively certain that the pink in my consciousness was my first moment of recognition, my first jerk from the symbiotic union with a world devoid of shapes and differences. I believe, in fact, that the consciousness of blue – the blue that was me – matured inside my spinning wheel of learning only as a consequence of my effort to determine pink's nature.

My tale about pink exasperates Jelena, because it belongs to that category of experiences she resentfully calls "your twiddle-twaddle", attempting to conceal her fear of the unknowable behind a façade of disdain. Jelena does believe in the original reality of my first sensation, but she stubbornly claims that the "primordial pink" I invented subsequently, is the fruit of my mature intellect and not of my earliest memories. Because she is scared of the inconceivable, Jelena tries hard to present herself as a pragmatic, geometrically predictable, unimaginative being. According to her, I am the dreamer, I imagine things, you see, while she is some sort of phlegmatic algebra professor who trusts only the palpable and the mathematically provable. She has succeeded in deceiving others, of course, but it is nothing other than a silly, childish game of burying-the-head-in-the-sand when she insists upon her fake presentation with *me*. Such nonsense! She looks straight at me and playacts stubbornly, conscious that I know as well as her why she

35

is doing it. At times, I let her. I don't say anything. Other times, I make it clear that I know everything:

"You're afraid, aren't you?"

"I am not afraid of anything."

"Palm reading and Black Magic."

"I have no idea what you mean."

"I mean precisely that: you're afraid of knowing what I mean even when I am not saying anything. And you do know."

"I find you annoying, you and your 'symbiotic communion'," she answered with scorn, though a scorn which could not comfort her nor convince me.

To Jelena, our symbiotic closeness is dangerous precisely because it is inexplicable. Our supernatural mutual-mind-reading ability frightens her. Jelena knows that I know that she remembers blue the same way I remember pink, but the fear of our reciprocal clairvoyance, of new confirmations of the sameness of our inner experiences, prompts her to attack my every mention of the unknowable. She deliberately seeks the most banal explanations for the inexplicable, in which we are both involved.

She thus attributes our very particular brand of closeness entirely to our growing up together. All right. This is true, I never attempted denying it. I was six months old and Jelena eight months when they placed us in a common cot with a frilly valance. From that moment on, we were fed at the same time – one on the left and the other on the right breast of our wet nurse Simka, we rode together in a carriage for twins, we were even addressed together, so that "Jovanandjelena" were not two names joined with a hyphen, but rather one word which lost its meaning when divided into its components.

We were growing up alone. Completely alone. Just the two of us. Entirely left to one another. With no mother and stepmother, as was commonly known.

But, without father and stepfather – this was known only to us.

Stavra, destined to be father and mother to two infants, dealt with his predicament stoically, with the patience of a hero, and considering his meagre education and peasant origins – aristocratically, even nobly. The dignity of his bearing was rooted in his acceptance of his own tiller-of-the-soil origins. "Money makes the poor man rich but it does not make him a gentleman" – that's more or less the concise life philosophy of the millionaire Stavra Arandjelović.

It was always with pride that I watched Stavra as he attuned his rapport with the "gentlemen" (he deemed gentlemanly only those educated and courteous individuals among gentlemen) without any self-diminishment, revealing in his demeanour great awareness of hierarchy – an element so glaringly absent from our hastily constructed society. Remaining a peasant at heart, Stavra held gentility in high esteem and was always capable of distinguishing the authentic from the mimetic. There is nothing embarrassing, he believed, about being a peasant. What is unseemly is pretending to be a gentleman.

On one occasion, I read to him a couple of sentences from Grol's *Prewar Serbia*, knowing that he would relate to its message quite personally: "Though he was educated abroad and held many prestigious posts throughout his career, Milovan Janković remained a peasant in spirit to his last day, just as a century later, Voivoda Mišić and Milorad Drašković would. Most importantly, however, they did so with profound inner contentment." Stavra was particularly impressed by those last words. Though he rarely shows his emotions, Stavra simply could not conceal his excitement that time. He repeated the words several times: "with profound inner contentment . . . hmm . . . yes, yes . . . with profound inner contentment . . . "

This notion of peasanthood as the source of Stavra's moral stalwartness influenced our family's interactions in a rather odd manner. Jelena certainly didn't mention it in the Biography, but I dare say that Stavra's principal feature as father was that he remained utterly foreign to us, starting from our earliest childhood. Not for lack of love. Stavra definitely loved us, he always has, but in a peasantly rigid way. He expended few words, and what is more, he was uneasy with expressions of affection usually reserved for mothers; he simply had no means of showing his affection for us.

He didn't have the means, but he also didn't want to, as will soon become obvious. We were aware of that from a very early age. I remember that even before entering the first grade, Jelena and I observed with great interest how other children love their parents, noticing that we did not love Stavra the same way. Love him we did – though differently. It sounds contemptuous when stated, even more so when written, but it comes closest to the truth: we love Stavra as a trustworthy, devoted servant, primarily because our father and step-father treated us as – gentry. A nurse for a governess, freshly powdered behinds, French preschool, a pony to ride – these were all genteel advantages which Stavra gladly provided for his children. Owing to them, however, the children irrevocably crossed the border separating them from peasanthood.

During our childhood and especially when we grew up, Stavra treated us as people from another circle. We are his children, it is true, and he does love us and wishes to serve us faithfully, but our circle is simply out of bounds for him. He did everything to make us genteel, he was proud that we had become what gentlefolk are in his mind, although he knew that in such a way, he was distancing himself from us.

For instance, we would never address Stavra as "father" or "papa", but always by his name. We never confided in him. He never held me on his lap. Jelena – only very rarely. If he did caress Jelena's hair or hold her on his lap, he would do it in a rigid, slightly bewildered fashion, making her feel awkward as well. He never beat us. He never reprimanded us, even. He would leave that to our nannies and governesses.

In other words, we were never close. We grew up without a father. That we were conscious of it is confirmed by a conversation between Jelena and myself when we were thirteen or fourteen:

"Doesn't Stavra sound a bit formal when he talks to us?" Jelena asked.

"Yes, he only seems to let his hair down when he talks to Tinca and Milorad."

It happened thus that Jelena and I devoted all the intimacy we were capable of to one another. In French preschool, and later in school, we had many acquaintances, but never made any friends among the other children. Jelena hated girls; I hated boys. The girls were, by and large, whimpering, petulant brats, as Jelena liked to say, and the boys were loud and physically aggressive. We felt best and safest only when we returned home, closed the door of our room and devoted ourselves to amusements which naturally changed as we grew older but had one thing in common: they were always shared.

To this day, for instance, we often read the same book simultaneously, and I always have the bizarre impression that the book, circulating through two minds, duplicates itself, only to become one again through the course of our conversation. The first novel we read together, which I am certain was divided in our parallel minds and subsequently unified again in our discussion and even more so in the inferences beyond and beneath our spoken words, was *Quo Vadis?* We considered Eunice, Vinicius, Petronius' wisdom and Nero's orgies our common good, part of our mixed spiritual heritage.

Mixed substances can no longer be distinguished. The new product is Jelena's as well as mine – it exists in two identical copies, in her consciousness and in mine.

Here is obvious proof:

Right around the time we had completed the amalgamation of images from Sienkiewicz's novel, a certain Mister Petrangelli, Stavra's business acquaintance, had come to our home for lunch. As soon as we saw him, Jelena and I looked at each other and understood. The moment we found ourselves alone in a room, we exclaimed in a chorus:

"Petronius!"

Exchanging our impressions of Petronius, we had constructed the same image in our minds. We knew his facial traits, his very particular kind of lackadaisical hunch, the colour of his voice, a certain morally ill, quivery flaccidness of his cheeks – all the aspects of Petronius' exterior attributed to our Petronius not by Sienkiewicz but by Jelena and me. We had recognized the Petronius of our mingling imaginations.

Was this all just a manifestation of growing up together? Though she argues that it was, even Jelena knows that isn't entirely possible.

Many brothers and sisters grow up together but don't pour into one another like waves. What is more, Jelena and I are not even brother and sister.

What are we, then? Even in my intoxicated state, I lacked the courage to pose that question to Jelena. Perhaps writing about it will prove more fruitful.

Are we lovers?

Here, I glance at Bonehead to see if he's shocked and perturbed, 'cause let me tell you – this sentence blew me away when I first read it, five years ago. But lo and behold! Bonehead's fast asleep!

The poor baby got tired. He lost tons of blood and the transfusions at the clinic are always half-arsed. Shortages, they claim. Fucking shortages. What else is new?

His pretty face is all calm. He looks even more like a calf in his sleep. I walk over to the sofa and kiss that lamby-damby forehead of his. I'd kiss him when he's awake, but it doesn't seem right. I can't.

I put the manuscript back into the bag. I roam quietly around the kitchen and the room. Nothing to do. I've considered sitting there and just staring at Bonehead, but that's pretty sick. I can't possibly be such a moron . . . Pancakes! Maybe I'll make some pancakes? I go back to the kitchen, but I change my mind within seconds. So I turn around.

Finally, I decide to give Kojović a call. I've had his number for the past four years. Never used it. Classic "I'll do it today . . . I'll do it tomorrow . . . maybe he's dead? Maybe he moved?" syndrome. But what do you know? I dial and – the old geezer picks up. You know, promptly.

I'm so and so, calling regarding such and such a thing.

Anyway, that's how it all started. Reading Jovan's "Wretched Treatise" to Bonehead and conversing with Kojović in "The Blue Rider".

III

As Hanzy the clown from the "Circus Internazional" in Crikvenica would proclaim – "meine Damen und Herren", the time is ripe for the disclosure of the much talked about biography over which my grandmother and grandfather have drunkenly argued into the wee hours. It too was in the canvas bag, amongst Grandma Jelena's other papers.

What we've got here is obviously a carbon copy – you can tell from the way the letters pale towards the end. The manuscript is single spaced, typed on to two yellowed sheets of paper.

STAVRA ARANDJELOVIĆ
a biography

Stavra Arandjelović was born in 1885 in the village of Lelići. He was the fourth of seven children in a poor farming family. As the most gifted student in Lelići, following the completion of primary school, he went on to study at the middle school in Valjevo, working as a quiltmaker's apprentice. Determined to get his secondary school education, he moved to Belgrade. Working as the assistant to an attendant in the Pandjelova building, Stavra successfully graduated from the State Business School (during his years as a student there, the school changed its name to "Business Academy"). Of the one hundred and twenty students of mercantile laws and skills, two were members of the female sex. One of them, Senka Milišić, daughter of the iron merchant Ilija Milišić, had grown fond of the handsome Stavra, but the chances that her wealthy businessman father would allow his only daughter to marry a penniless pauper were very slim. However, in 1906, Ilija Milišić suddenly died and so, three years later, Stavra married Senka (owing, of course, to a soft-hearted mother and to Senka's own input) and Senka's substantial inheritance.

Though he was very successful in business, which shall be elaborated upon later, Stavra had less luck in the private matters of his life. As far as I know, my stepfather and his wife loved and respected one another but had no offspring for a long time. Then, in 1923, when they had all but lost hope, Senka became pregnant at age thirty-four. Their great joy was shortlived. Senka gave birth to a healthy boy named Jovan but she died in childbirth.

The life of my mother, Olivera Ljubisavljević, who would later become the second wife of the widower Stavra Arandjelović, was unfolding under entirely different circumstances. Olivera was the vain and spoiled only child of the famous business family Nerandžić whose wealth had endured for three generations and whose educational credits included the world's best universities. At a young age, she met Socrates Ljubisavljević, a businessman's son himself (his mother, who was Greek, had capital in the ship-building industry of the Costopoulos family from Thessaloniki). Their love was intense but brief, and the disappointment my mother suffered overwhelming though not unexpected. Following a grand ceremony in the Saborna church and a three-month honeymoon tour of the cosmopolitan centres of Europe, they settled in Belgrade. Soon thereafter, I was born. Four months after my arrival, the twenty-two-year-old Socrates and the twenty-four-year-old Olivera divorced. My mother married the thirty-eight-year-old industrialist Stavra Arandjelović just two months later.

The following year, burdened by depression, my mother committed suicide. Stavra Arandjelović was left alone with two infants, Jovan from his first marriage and his step daughter Jelena, who grew up loved and cared for, a fact to which this text acts as grateful testimony.

Stavra began his business career with a small but sound capital. When the late Milišić's creditors, ranging from wealthy foreign businesses to Serbian peasants, paid off the last of their debts, Milišić's widow and daughter were left with capital valued at 236,000 dinars.

In the year 1909, such a sum could be considered both small and large. Small for someone spendthrift and idle but large for the hardworking newcomer craving success and riches. By helping out in the export department of Belgrade's Chamber of Commerce in business with Greece and Turkey, Stavra acquired a name among businessmen and was elected Chamber of Commerce representative at the Township Treasury Board.

However, the one truly crucial step in the business career of Stavra Arandjelović was his decision to enter a partnership with the sons of the candlemaker Kosta Ílić from Vlasotinci. The two brothers owned a cord and textile factory in Leskovac, and the three of them started a modern textile industry in Belgrade. With their own capital and the investment of the Budapest branch of the Serbian Bank totalling 250.000 dinars in gold, the three partners purchased the textile factory of Evgenij Mihel including all its buildings and machinery. They founded a firm by the name of "The Royal Serb Authorized Factory of Woollen Textiles".

The ambitions of the owners were rather great – they wanted to launch a modern European textile business for the production of all kinds of textiles. With that in mind, they founded a stock company with a starting capital of 1,000,000 dinars in gold. The company fell into temporary financial trouble during the Balkan Wars and interrupted production completely during the First World War. Following liberation and unification, despite the damage done to the machinery and to the buildings, the partnership was granted security and reparation loans from domestic banks and embarked upon the most contemporary form of textile production. The running power of the production machinery of the "Royal Serb Authorized Factory of Woollen Textiles" amounted to 750 ks, the spinning mill had 13 celfactors with a total of 2,830 spindles, the textile department had 754 looms while its 700 workers produced 300,000 kilograms of yarn and 4 million metres of fabric a year. I must also mention that the salaries and wages of the employees of Stavra Arandjelović's plant increased from 625,000 dinars in 1935 to more than 2 million dinars for more or less the same number of employees in 1940.

After the arrival of German troops in Belgrade, the new authorities took over the factory and changed its production entirely. Like all other businesses useful to the war industry, Stavra Arandjelović's plant also produced, under orders, for the needs of the German army.

Powerless to change the state of things, yet driven by a patriotic conscience, Stavra Arandjelović withdrew from business and stopped going to the factory as well as to his office in the first half of 1941.

He was arrested on November 2nd 1944. We do not know why.

Jelena Ljubisavljević-Arandjelović

This is bull. Grandpa Jovan was right. This biography thing is completely barking.

"Isn't that right, my dear Bonehead?" I ask Bonehead.

"Sure is. This kind of thing wouldn't help with any authority, much less with the Communists."

Bonehead is right. But he's wrong too. Had Jovan and Jelena really been squabbling over the damn biography, Bonehead would be right. No question. That sort of biography would've only buried the poor man six feet deeper. What I'm saying is – those barbarians may be this or that but one thing they are sure of is how to score brownie points in Marxism. From the biography, it's clear as day that Stavra was a "dirty Capitalist". That's all they gave a shit about. To quote my friend, King Ubu: "In the interest of the growth of my own wealth, I will kill all the noblemen and confiscate their properties." A hell of a healthy principle. And pretty durable, if you know what I mean. So, basically, it was Stavra's problem that he had property.

But, BIG but, that isn't the point. Jovan and Jelena weren't arguing over that. Something else is at stake here. Maybe we'd better fill you in, Bonehead and I, on our little secret, but *nein*. Suffer. The truth should be discovered gra-dual-ly. I'm not taking a course on Archer for nothing. So, we'll take it nice and slowly. I am by orientation an illiterate writer, but, as the reader (*if* there ever is one, which is to say, if Djura manages to stick this "Wretched Treatise" under anybody's nose) can see for himself, I am not an uneducated writer.

"Isn't that right, Bonehead?"

"Right!" says he.

44

You know, Bonehead is like a human miracle, I kid you not. The other day, while I was at class, this macho man from Moslavina in all of his limping splendour made the bed and even shoved the dirty sheets into the wash! What the hell? – this I said when I got home. I felt pretty embarrassed letting him do my housework, but he wouldn't let go of that mop and bucket: "No, no, out of my way, I'll take care of it. You just sit there. Besides, Jela, you couldn't fix a thing in the house if your bloody life depended on it." And you know what? He's right. The little fucker is right. I just can't.

And since he casually remarked that I couldn't cook anything except hard-boiled eggs without provoking minor cataclysms, Bonehead has taken the matter into his own hands. French toast, pancakes, stuffed peppers, homemade bread – you name it – the guy's cooking like there's no tomorrow!

My little prodigy from Moslavina.

IV

I could've zapped someone this morning. Honest. I mean, I should've. At least those three. Four if you count Bonehead.

First, the bearded cow at the reception desk of the clinic. Bearded and hairy-legged, to be precise. The cigarette is not just glued to her mouth – it's cemented there.

Anyway, we come in, we sit down. Two and a half hours later, Tyrant Face is finally calling our names:

"Bogdan Bilogorac!"

We're fucking delirious with joy. We're so ecstatic we could puke. Bogdan the wounded hero leaps forth. I follow. The beauty in the window exclaims:

"Tut, tut, Bogdan. M'fraid it ain't gonna work . . ."

"What do you mean it ain't? What's wrong?" I ask.

"You're not a resident, Bogdan."

"So?" – me again.

"You need certification from the Refugee Centre in Nusiceva Street."

"For a bandage change?"

"For every medical service."

"But you've never asked for it before."

"That's because I'm a good person."

This is where I said to her, in the most gracious manner possible:

"You're good enough for the fucking pound, you furry ape."

I exited the waiting room calm and dignified.

We waited for the certification at the Refugee Centre till we were fucking ultra-marine blue in the face. The next day, we're back at the clinic. We were among the first to submit our papers, and as expected, she called our names last.

This time, I'm not even getting near the reception desk; I may be tempted to commit a criminal act. The cow glances at the documents and says:

"Pretty good, pretty good. Now, did you bring the gauze and the bandages, Bogdan?"

"No, I didn't."

"And how do you expect us to bandage you?"

"Why the fuck didn't you tell us yesterday that you had run out of bandages?" I screech.

"Because we *weren't* out yesterday, darlin'" – the cigarette is still glued to her yapper like a fucking breathing device.

I didn't inflict any injuries upon her. I merely ordered Führer-style:

"When I come back next time, I wanna see that facial fur shaved, understood?"

We get outside, and Bonehead, the sweetheart that he is, tries to comfort me. "We'll go to McDonald's for a burger, if you want," he says.

"Fine. But first, we'll go to a private doc for this bandage change."

So we pay a little visit to Dr Cvetković on Birčaninova Street. And there, it's capitalism at its finest. You know – airconditioned, disinfected, airtight, leak-proof, that kind of thing. The secretary, a sexy babe with tits up to here and no moustache, offers us magazines to read. They have bandages, gauze, everything; they even have a doctor. In-fucking-credible.

We're finished in no time. Good-bye. Good-bye. Come back again. Sure.

I ask the babe how much we owe them and she goes:

"Four and a half thousand."

"I'm sorry, did I hear you right? Did you say *thousand*?"

"Uh-huh."

Charming young woman.

"This dear young patriot receives six thousand a month," I said, "for everything."

"Believe me," she says, "the material alone costs us three thousand. The blockade, you know."

This obviously isn't our day. Bonehead digs out three red ones from his pocket. I give the only red one I had, plus three blue ones. I say:

"That's all we have – we're two hundred short."

"That's all right. Bring it next time," she says.

Next time?! Right. I didn't deck these two either, but I did proclaim on our way out:

"We'll drop by on our way to Hawaii."

So we've got no burgers, we've got no dough, no nothing. Ever since those fucking sanctions started, nothing's been coming in the mail from scumbag. And to top that, nobody's paying anybody anymore. The "Mag" published eight of my photos, plus I spent a month slaving away for the National Theatre and the "Modern" and nobody paid me a penny. Maybe we should join the strikers. No kidding. At least they get free food. I inform Bonehead of this perk. He replies, disheartened:

"As soon as I'm a bit more up and about, Jela, I'll get a job unloading boxes, so we'll have a little extra."

He was so sweet I wanted to kiss him right then and there but I quickly took control. No shit, it takes more than that to win me over.

"Screw money," I said after little deliberation. "When you get better, we'll devote ourselves to badminton, that's what we'll do. You know what badminton is?"

"Of course I know what badminton is!"

"Oh, silly me. How could I forget! That's the national sport in your transequatorial hometown."

"Oh come on! You're kiddin', right?"

He says that a lot – the "Oh come on, you're kiddin'". He manages to say it in a very unique way. Kind of shyly. So sweetly you want to die. Some Serbian artilleryman we have here, eh?

On Terazije Street, in front of the "Kasina" restaurant, piles of Moslavinian farts are standing around, twiddling their thumbs. Why Moslavinian, you ask? How do I know, you ask? I have two words for you: dress code. Some of its classic features are: the hat, soaked in grease marks; for some kind of Indiana Jones effect the white

48

shirt, buttoned up all the way, concealing the enchanting hairy chest and endowing the body with an air of mystical unavailability; the crumpled collar, adding the essential element of nonchalance and free-spiritedness. Then of course, there is the blue jacket, exquisitely well matched with the brown trousers (the reverse combination is also available), and finally, the coquettishly dusty shoes with one of the laces inevitably torn and tied back together in a knot. Stunning, isn't it? There's gotta be some kind of a specialist boutique that caters for these guys. I mean, I've never seen a suit made up of a blue jacket and brown trousers, have you? Whenever I see two bicoloured guys like that, I start wondering why the hell they don't trade trousers, so at least they're in one colour. In-fucking-credible.

"Are these guys friends of yours?" I ask Bonehead.

"Which guys?"

I point to one of the groups. After he's examined them carefully, he goes:

"Not mine." (Dramatic pause.) "Ours," he says.

I look at him. He's giggling.

"They're Serbs, they're our guys," he adds.

"You're kidding, right?"

"Well, it's my turn, eh?"

We passed right by McDonald's.

"Are we goin' into this one?" Bonehead said, as we approached the cafeteria of the philosophy school.

"Nope. We're going to the philology department. They got better fodder."

At the entrance to the philology building, I decide to give him motherly advice about world affairs:

"No Serbing around, understand?"

"OK, OK, I know."

"If anyone asks, you injured your leg playing polo with the Duke of Kent."

"You're kiddin', right?"

"No, I'm not."

49

Inside, in the amphitheatre, the atmosphere's sort of drowsy. Few revolutionaries. Twenty, maybe thirty in all. Some fat old guy is screeching into the mike: Milošević, Bolshevism, the violent type, our mythic past, our shitty present, tralala . . .

"Who's this guy?" I ask the tart next to me.

"An anti-war activist."

Hmm . . . intriguing . . .

"Postmodernist?" I ask.

"No, structuralist."

I grab Bonehead by the hand and lead him to the cafeteria. Fresh bread, meat, tomato. A feast for the hungry.

"I'm kind of embarrassed to do this, Jela," he says, chewing like his mouth is full of fucking plutonium.

I roll my eyes. Could have dumped him right then and there.

We get home:

"Do you still want me to read you Jovan's thing?" I ask.

"Yeah, OK."

"You're not gonna fall asleep like last time?"

"I ain't gonna. I'm stronger now."

"When you get bored, yell."

"Don't you worry about a thing. Just read on."

So here we go. From where we left off:

JOVAN (2)

Was this all a manifestation of our growing up together? Though she argues that it was, even Jelena knows that isn't entirely possible. Many brothers and sisters grow up together but don't pour into one another like waves. What is more, Jelena and I aren't even brother and sister.

What are we, then? Even in my intoxicated state, I lacked the courage to pose that question to Jelena. Perhaps writing about it will prove more fruitful.

Are we lovers?

* * *

"Holy shit! This is gettin' serious!" shrieked Bonehead. I paid no attention to this insightful interjection:

In 1936, on the second day of Christmas (Jelena was about to turn fourteen in a few days; my own birthday was in two months' time), we both came down with the 'flu. We weren't seriously ill, but our fevers were high enough to make rest in bed necessary. At that time, we did have separate rooms but we had temporarily moved my bed into Lena's room so as to better bear up with the boredom of our days of indisposition.

I cannot remember why we were alone in the house on the second day of Christmas. It is likely that our governess, Miss Melanija, had left for Novi Sad to spend the holidays with her relatives, and that Stavra, who considered holidays a waste of time, had made up some sort of unpostponable work assignment. After all, we were grown-up enough to take care of ourselves.

As boredom set in, we tried thinking of games to play. It wasn't getting dark yet – it must have been no later than three or four o'clock. The space between our beds was filled with scattered bits of fancy wrapping paper; on our night tables stood woven baskets decorated with evergreen twigs and golden hay piled high with oranges, whole hazelnuts and walnuts, bananas, sweets in different-coloured wrappings, dates, prunes and figs. The smell of oranges and liqueur-filled chocolates permeated the air.

We had decided to try out the game "Monopoly" – one of our Christmas gifts. I recall the most valuable properties that the game offered for exchanges or for sale, providing one had the money, of course, and the luck: The Ilica in Zagreb, Hotel Kvarner in Abacia, The Yugoslav State Railroad, the Belgrade Mortgage House, the palaces Kiki and Riunione, the firm Elektro-Makiš . . . In order to play the game and simultaneously follow the doctor's advice of lying horizontally, I had had to move into Lena's bed. We rolled the dice on the top surface of the Monopoly box. We bought and sold, making transactions, investing capital, going bankrupt etc . . . Nothing but the game itself was on our minds.

At least, that is what I remember. I am writing as I remember it. What I don't know, I don't write. Simply recording events. So, moving on:

I don't exactly know how and when our interest in the game waned. Perhaps we grew tired of playing it. Perhaps it was the onset of darkness or our rising fevers that interrupted us. At any rate, we threw the board and the pieces down to the floor and lay motionless under the same comforter, watching the festively red glow of the fire inside our tile furnace.

Suddenly, I heard silence. One of the days in our communal life which Jelena staunchly refuses to discuss is that second day of Christmas. Despite her refusal, I am certain that at that moment, she also heard silence. The silence of dormant Belgrade, of the decorated horse-drawn sleigh soundlessly gliding down the street, the silence of Senjak – our neighbourhood – the silence of our yard buried beneath the deep snow criss-crossed with pathways to the garage and to the street, the silence of our empty house and finally, the loudest, near palpable silence of our room.

The last time she allowed me to mention that evening, sometime around last October, when the battle for the liberation of Belgrade was raging in the streets, Jelena told me that she did not remember the conversation we had. I accepted her memory-lapse excuse and tried reminding her nonetheless:

"You must remember! I said to you 'You've grown breasts, Lena,' and you said 'Yes,' remember? Then I said 'I got hair, down below, and you replied 'Me too'. How can you not remember that?"

The roar of the artillery cannonade was coming from the general direction of the main highway, while some machine-gun battles were already being waged quite near our house in Krunska Street. Jelena and I sat huddled together under a blanket in the basement, my arm wrapped around her shoulders. Having heard my question, she nervously moved aside so that the blanket fell between our two bodies, and said:

"I don't remember. It's all rubbish. We were children."

Whether it was all rubbish and whether we were children is

debatable still. But that Jelena remembers is a solid fact. She remembers. She remembers as well as I do, neither better, nor worse. The image of the Christmas evening of 1936 is distant in our consciousness, just as the image of Christ's birth in Bethlehem may be. But it's alive, more alive than any reality currently forcing its deceptive irrefutability upon our senses.

Both of us remember everything. Both of us do.

Lying sideways with my cheek pressed against the pillow and my eyes fixed upon the fire in the tile furnace, I said:

"I would like to see them."

An entire minute passed, maybe more, in complete immobility and quiet, before Jelena sat up and started taking off her nightgown. I too sat up and helped her drag out the lower part of her gown from underneath herself. Against the lugubrious red of the fire, her paleness suddenly lit up like a second source of light. She seemed so white!

I don't think that anybody has skin as white as Jelena's. It is impossible to confuse the whiteness of Jelena's skin with any colour on this colourful planet, and that is precisely why its perfect uniqueness evades words. What could one compare it with? White as – what? White as Jelena's skin.

"Look," she said as she sat there naked, twisting towards me to better show off her grown breasts. On the two rounded surfaces, her disproportionately large brown nipples stood out against the whiteness.

I wanted to say something. I wanted to tell her that they were wonderful, but I didn't say anything for one of two, or both reasons simultaneously: I could not gather the right words to describe the beauty of her untouched breasts, nor could I have propelled those unfound words through my throat, which was gripped with strange excitement. My hand reached towards her nipples, moving softly from one to the other, while the rest of me sat there, bewitched by the sensation of touching, intoxicated to such a degree that I cannot determine whether this holy event lasted an eternity or whether Jelena quickly pulled away:

"Don't. It tickles," she said, visibly excited, though scared of her excitement and of the rapidity with which it grew. And though she had pulled away from my hand, she didn't wish to interrupt the flow of the revelation, so she abruptly pulled the comforter down, and quickly lay down again, with her hands clasped behind her neck.

"See, mine have grown too," she said, pointing with her eyes towards the furry triangle whose apex disappeared between her gripping thighs. She didn't object when I placed my hand on it nor when I later used my other hand to caress her dark, erect nipples. I was boiling, yet I felt, beneath my hands, that her skin was also heating up. I felt the opening between her legs and entered it with my fingers. She squeaked, softly.

I remember asking her all at once, in a whisper:

"Do you want to see mine?" I didn't wait for her answer; I simply took off my pyjama pants and knelt on the bed, facing her, so that she could see it. She first felt it with her fingertips and then proceeded to squeeze it with the palm of her hand.

"I want your hand down here too," she whispered back.

I did as she asked.

At that precise moment, we exploded.

It was quite similar to what would happen in my sleep, though a hundred times more sensual. I thought I was dying. At age fourteen, I am quite certain of it, I experienced a sensual death. Sometimes, I seriously regret that I did not physically die at that moment. Even today, I best comprehend the concept of death when I link it to the debauched craze of our early adolescence.

We lay in complete silence, near one another. Consciousness returned to both of us in phases, like cold waves. It returned us to life, to the reality of our room. I am not sure how long it lasted. I do know that Jelena broke the silence.

"That's your sperm," she said, feeling the liquid on her breasts. Her words sounded more fact-confirming than interrogative.

I felt deathly fragile, muted. The use of words struck me as somehow unseemly. Following another long silence, Jelena spoke again:

"Let's go and get washed in the bathroom. Somebody could turn up."

I didn't want to move.

54

"There's nobody in the house," I said, but Jelena got up and offered her hand:

"Let's go, little one," she said, smiling.

Never before nor after the fateful Christmas evening did Jelena call me "little one" and never did she smile at me the way she did then. I tried interpreting both "little one" and the smile more than a hundred times, but never could. Accustomed to noticing and understanding (with no conscious intention) every gesture, every flicker of emotion ever to appear in Jelena, I was at odds for the very first time with the workings of her head and her soul. But, whichever angle of approach I may take, and I've taken many in the last seven years, I always arrive at the same, senseless conclusion: Jelena's "Let's go, little one" and her smile actually reflected a feeling of pity. I know that my conclusion isn't rational; I haven't disclosed a single reason as to why Jelena may have felt pity for me. Nevertheless, I simply cannot interpret her strange words and her kind smile differently. For, in the course of the next week, or should I say – the next three years and more, Jelena and I lingered in a state of delirium, torn apart by sexual desire and by our guilt for having fallen under its spell.

DESIRE

Our desire was now total and absolute; only now, in retrospect, do I understand why it had to be so. The novelty of it, the revelation can certainly be counted in, but the main secret lay concealed in the fourteen-year-old Jelena's erotic wondrousness.

Jelena's early girlhood was devoid of sensual significance. Early youth, in general, is by nature non-erotic. Since I knew Jelena inside-out, I knew that she was frightened of what was happening to her body, despite Miss Melanija's stiff and evasive explications. Jelena had just grasped that sex is a dangerous secret, that her breasts are a wonder. The mysterious slit between her legs, blood – those were the subjects of the timid adolescent's first confused evaluations.

But the moment her sexuality, full of mysterious hazes, transformed into a living craze of the senses under the sudden effect of physical contact, a stage began in the life of Jelena-the-woman, in which

Jelena-the-promiscuous-child gained the strength of an erotic monster. This monster was capable of devastating not only my mind but the mind of any other with her incredible combination of innocent juven-escence and awakened eroticism. I am not arguing that my disturbed mind was not subject to sexual frenzy as well. But what were minds doing amongst us savages? There was only room for madness. For our own, mutual madness. For Jelena, the secret disturbed on that holiday evening, restive until that moment, as if touched by the magic wand, became the source of the greatest pleasures. It became an open, flar-ingly bright desire, a precipice and a maelstrom; during Christmas of 1936, Jelena became extraordinarily awakened.

The eroticism of the mature woman can never possess such power. I am convinced of it, though I haven't had any sexual experiences with women. The eroticism of the mature woman must certainly pale with overuse, much like coloured silk does in the bright sun; her sensuality cannot, by nature, be shrouded in a veil of wonder, discovery, un-repeatability, cloaking the young woman who still bears the freshest memory of herself as child.

We lived in a state of delirium, and I am surprised to this day that nobody ever noticed our near-total befuddlement. We spent our days waiting for the rare opportunity to slip out of the sight of other house-hold members, but only when we became conspirators did we realize to what extent (and how closely) our lives were supervised. Miss Melanija still lived with us and slept in the room between mine and Jelena's, thus nights were not suited for our secret encounters. We spent our mornings in school and afternoons in the company of the governess or in her immediate vicinity.

A few times, still, in constant fear of being discovered, hence fully clothed and ready to stop at any instant, we caressed one another. Jelena would lean against the tile furnace (we had discovered that the heat it generated increased our excitement and that positioning ourselves behind it would give us enough time to straighten up before being seen by the person whose steps we would hear in the corridor a second or two before they entered the room). I would lift her leg with my left hand while using my right hand (as I had done at Christmastime but this time without taking off her panties), to stimulate her clitoris. She would force both hands inside my trousers. We always came very quickly, always in a panic. Breathless and terrified. We longed for another Christmas evening, though we knew that it could happen only under a favourable and rare set of circumstances: we waited for the Saturday afternoon when Miss Melanija's visit to a friend in Zemun, the maid's day off and Stavra's absence coincided.

That day came. Such a Saturday afternoon came and we took advantage of it. The chauffeur and the cook were very unlikely to come to our room; in fact they never had, but we took no risks – we locked ourselves in the bathroom.

We took off all our clothes.

I reached to turn off the light but Jelena stopped me.

"You were more beautiful in the dark," I said.

"Still. Leave it on," she replied.

We had become lovers.

Real lovers.

Secret ones.

GUILT

Without the presence of guilt in each and every one of its cells, sexual desire would be entirely different from the one experienced by Jelena and myself. We were guilty. Ever since that first Christmas evening. With each subsequent secret union, we were even guiltier. Both of us were, though Jelena evidently had a harder time coming to terms with her sinfulness. We knew without a doubt that we were engaged in something dirty, dangerous, punishable and abnormal. Though I was not capable of doing so at the time, I shall now try to deconstruct our guilt.

In its first layer resided fear. Sex between adults contains a forbidden and punishable part. Sex between children – we still thought of ourselves as children – was something that needed to be kept secret at any price, even if that price were our own deaths. Stavra would despise us. Our relatives would be appalled. Everyone in school would turn against us. The whole city would despise us, possibly the whole country, the whole of Europe.

* * *

I awake in a cold sweat. I had a dream: our bathroom is crowded with people. I do not recognize the majority of them, but I am able to discern relatives, friends from school, professors. Stavra is somewhere in the background. He is pushing through the crowd with all his strength but he can't seem to get through. In the bath filled to the brim with boiling water, Jelena and I are copulating shamelessly. We are both aware, in a manner possible only in dreams, that everything would be resolved in a positive manner if only we interrupted our shameful, possessed act. We do want to interrupt it. Both of us do, intensely. But we can't. That fuels our panic. The guilt becomes unbearable.

I wake up.

I feel saved.

At least, temporarily.

There was another fear – Jelena's fear of pregnancy, which was my fear as well, naturally. A moustached Russian Jew from the eighth year, Belov was his name, Yevgeni Belov, had procured me some condoms. Still, the fear didn't dissipate, as it had no basis in reality. After all, we thought, the Virgin Mother had become pregnant without engaging in shameful acts. God could punish us despite our conscientious use of "Olagum" condoms. We were in fact absolutely certain that God would punish us, but the certainty of the punishment did not scare us; on the contrary, strangely but effectively, it attenuated our guilt: given that our deserved punishment was imminent, our actions were forgivable to a degree.

"We will be punished, Jovan, I am sure of it." She used these words as consolation, since the imminence of the punishment established an equilibrium with the sin.

At this time, Miss Melanija, our governess, was no longer living with us. Every evening, as soon as the household was enveloped in silence, I would crawl into Jelena's bed. As soon as we awoke, the thought of punishment was on our minds. The punishment had to be quite grave, we argued, for such was our sin – we were brother and sister.

"We are not brother and sister," I would tell her, referring to the book of Leviticus – *"None of you shall approach anyone near of kin* – emphasizing those three words – *to uncover nakedness. I am the Lord."*

"The nakedness of your sister, the daughter of your father and your mother" – do you hear that, Jelena, I would tell her – *"should she be born in the house or away from it, you shall not uncover it."*

Not even the Word of God could dissuade Jelena.

"You know that we are brother and sister," she would say, and I knew that she was right.

We are indeed brother and sister. We are more than that. We are twins. We are Siamese twins. We are one.

The fervour of our desperate nocturnal encounters gradually waned; confusion and fear grew. Guilt, more overwhelming than ever before, took us over completely. I felt crushed, though not surprised, when one night, on her way to her room, Jelena declared:

"Don't come tonight."

"Why?"

"Because."

She didn't need to explain further. I had understood everything.

The frequency of our nightly visitations decreased. Only occasion-ally would I convince her to let me crawl under her covers, and even on such occasions, the sex was more bitter than pleasurable. More specifically, we were not capable of separating the two. Desire became bitterness. Jelena regularly cried during these harsh sessions. Yet she grew more (oh dear Lord, if you exist indeed, you must testify to this) and more virginally white, more sinfully soft under my touch than ever before!

On her seventeenth birthday, looking straight into my eyes, she said:

"We shall never sleep together again. Never."

I knew it would be so. I knew that was the final verdict.

The realization that our sexual conspiracy had ended devastated me. I had begun suffering from an illness, which, I later found out, was known as narcolepsy in psychiatric terms, and manifested itself in an insatiable need to sleep. Had it not been for Jelena, who energetically, sometimes begging, sometimes cursing, got me out of bed each morning, I would have spent my days and nights in a state of delirium halfway between sleep and consciousness.

I had stopped reading. Now, I am not a hard-working person. I am much too relaxed and insufficiently ambitious to be a diligent worker. I am inquisitive, however, and was thus always very fond of reading. I don't think that I ever read a book because I had to, but I always found books which I *genuinely wanted* to read.

Not during the months of my delirium.

Thus, having lost the desire to read, I had lost the motivation for any type of action. I would sometimes spend a stretch of several days in a kind of perplexity, seeing only the faintest outlines of people, barely knowing who I was talking to, whom I was meeting. Reality became dubious. I wasn't quite sure I existed.

"Do we exist?" I asked Jelena, just as I might ask her "Is today Thursday?"

Perhaps today is Thursday, and perhaps it isn't. Perhaps we exist and perhaps somebody is dreaming that we are now doing and thinking what they are dreaming.

In a psychological state such as that, I had no desire for anything, absolutely anything. Not even a naked Jelena before my eyes. Jelena was concerned about my narcolepsy, confusion, apathy, and she fought bravely against these worrisome symptoms of a neurosis. In an attempt to divert my attention away from my sick fixations, she talked to me tirelessly, nursed me, did everything to please me and tried to revive my comatose interest in what used to be our favourite games. Mostly with limited or no success. Once she suggested that we see Dr Vujić or Dr Jekić.

"To tell him everything?" I asked, ready to do that too in my state of sick indifference.

Jelena didn't answer my question, and she never repeated her suggestion again.

We had stopped talking entirely about our romantic memories. It was as if they no longer existed. Only much later, following my successful rehabilitation, which lasted a long time and went through many phases, did I attempt initiating conversations and getting answers to questions Jelena had banished from her mind. But in the most acute period of my somnambulism, not even I exhibited the desire to reminisce about our erotic frenzy. I would even say that the first symptoms of my convalescence were phenomenally real erotic dreams in which I was making love to Jelena once again.

I have the same dreams today. Regularly. Therefore – I am healthy. Every night. Seven years after our last encounter. Four years after having overcome an acute psychosis.

So, today – what are Jelena and I to each other today?

Are we lovers?

When she finished writing Stavra's biography and asked, looking into my eyes:

"Would you like to read it?" it was clear to me that our symbiotic union stood before tribulations of a different sort but equal in depth to the ones of seven years ago. Consumed with fear and panic, I replied:

"No." A cowardly and punctuated "No" it was, though I knew that our encoded talk of the biography quickly needed to be translated into talk of the real subject:

Krsman.

Of the barbarian who, following a corporate break-in of Communists into Belgrade, was now singularly breaking into Jelena's and my life. *If* he is, I thought. *If* this lunatic fear of loss isn't fogging up my brain and taking my clairvoyance down the wrong path.

However, neither my panic over Jelena's resoluteness in undertaking the salvation of Stavra in a partnership with Krsman, nor my understanding of the meaning of such resoluteness was accidental. I was absolutely unprepared for the circumstances I had never hitherto encountered in my life with Jelena. I felt, I sensed that something was happening between Jelena and the barbarian, something that never, I repeat, *never* before happened between Jelena and any other man.

Jelena had never, ever expressed any interest whatsoever in any of her numerous admirers, save falsely, so that she and I could amuse ourselves by playing a game I had invented and named "Cat and Mouse". It was for the purposes of this game that towards the end of

1943, we began attending parties which we had been invited to by our peers, relatives and acquaintances from the university. Those parties had the tendency of being rather drunken and licentious. The two of us weren't behind our generation in drinking, but we never allowed ourselves to become drunk in public. Usually, one of us would warn the other that it was time to withdraw and we would complete our drinking bout alone, in the privacy of our room.

Naturally, Jelena was always, with no exception, the centre of male attention, and by equal measure, the object of the female half of the company's unconcealed hatred. It must be said (and I emphasize this not only because it is my beloved Lena I am talking about but because it is the simple truth) that she always withstood both types of attention with the disengaged hauteur of some close cousin to a Roman emperor. I admired the skill with which she managed to communicate to her individual admirer what she pretended to try to hide at any cost: that she is truly bored and that she is making a great effort to appear kind and high-spirited in the face of her suitor's aggressive courting. Worthy of even greater esteem was the icy stare and the murderous sarcasm, employed (like a ping-pong bat, reaching in perfect backhands and forehands) chiefly to shield her against the poisonous arrows of female malice. That is, providing the Empress Jelena acknowledged her rivals at all – generally only in situations in which they became overly irritating. I would ask myself: Where did she learn that? How did she perfect her skill so? I realized with time, however, that the skill was not something one could learn and perfect – it was a gift from God to a very few chosen beauties.

The most adorable aspect of Jelena's other game – the "Vanity Game" – was the lack of underlying narcissism in her self-presentation. I wish to say that Jelena never presented herself as unconquerable, impenetrable, with the intention of fuelling the desire or tickling the egos of her male intriguers. No. On the contrary, she had invented the "Vanity Game" so that the tedious parties we attended would pass in amusement for the two of us, both while the game lasted, as well as afterwards, in the privacy of our home, when we retold each event, laughing at its comical turn.

Jelena was also the main protagonist of the game "Cat and Mouse". When I would evaluate an acute suitor as being appropriate for a mouse, I would discreetly, so that it was visible only to her, make hand gestures representing the leaping of a cat. With the fingers of my other hand, I would mime the motions of a tiny mouse in flight. This was the sign that Jelena should give her wooer hope. Not too much, so that he wouldn't go berserk, but just enough to encourage him to make a fool of himself. The most admirable aspect of Jelena's flawless and masterful travesty was the dosage: the accelerations and the decelerations, the interplay between stimulating and obstructing, between leaps and screeching halts; a game whose minutest aspect she supervised brilliantly, never revealing for a moment to her cavalier the many ways in which he was being ridiculed.

Jelena enjoyed the game indeed, but never more than me. It is essential to establish that. It is essential to know that I had invented the game, that I was the one prompting Jelena to give her suitors semblances of hope. It wasn't a question of any jealousy on my part. *Au contraire* – the "Vanity Game" helped me overcome the fact that we were no longer lovers, and I knew that Jelena played the game primarily for my sake, aware of the fact that she was mitigating the pain of my unstitched wound. The "Cat and Mouse" game simply compounded the beneficial effects of the "Vanity Game". In Jelena's pseudo-amorous shenanigans, the two of us were partners, the sole initiates in the secret game, thus alone and together against the whole world. I was aware of that. I knew exactly what was taking place inside her beautiful head – the way the two of us know what the other thinks, feels and communicates without expending a single word.

Even the time when she went further than was customary in the "Cat and Mouse" game by going to the movies with Siniša Ristić, a good-looking, slickly combed nitwit with a tandem, attending a party with him (to which I had not been invited), and letting him kiss her good night at our gate – even then, I was perfectly calm, because I knew that Jelena was doing it for me: she was testing the degree of my recovery, testing my readiness to withstand the loss of the sexual aspect of our intimacy. She was upset when I told her I was beginning to discern the purpose of her experiment. When she went on a date with Siniša for the third or fourth time, subtly informing me of that fact, I replied calmly and cheerfully, since I did feel calm and cheerful:

"Lena, I'm all right."

"What exactly do you mean?"

"I feel no discomfort."

"What sort of discomfort?"

"Abdominal. Cardiovascular. Neuromuscular – hence, no discomfort of any sort."

"Witty. Quite witty," she replied, and stuck out her tongue.

She still went on her date, but it was to be the last one. As I had penetrated to the heart of her secret game, no sense remained in playing it any longer.

Why am I then lending so much time and space to it all in this journal? Because I was feeling, because I was sensing rather than deducing rationally that with Krsman, it no longer was a game! I didn't know what it was. But in the way she spoke of him, ridiculed him, avoided my gaze, in the hidden nervousness of her sarcasm, there appeared something which never hitherto existed in Jelena's treatment of men.

And here, right here, just around the corner from "Jelena's treatment of men", Bonehead came on to me – I mean full speed! Playtime!

As I was reading the last few lines, he got up from the sofa he was lying on, came behind my armchair and casually stuck his hand between my tits. I thought to myself:

"Praise God – he remembered!"

In romance novels, they tend to write things like: "Jelena heaved a sigh of relief". Well, you get my meaning – I don't know if I sighed or not, but the bells were ringing, the alarms were going off, definitely. Why? Because I'd been wondering for days if Bonehead wanted to fuck me or not. I look at him and I wonder. At one point I'm thinking – sure he wants me, he just doesn't want to come across as thankless. I know how their minds work, those Boneheads from Moslavina – like, it's uncool – I brought him home, I'm feeding him, nursing him, tralala . . . Other times I'm thinking – shit, it's never even crossed his mind! Who am I kidding? My big arse just doesn't do it for him. My charming blackheads disgust him. He likes me – as a friend. I'm sick and fucking tired of those who like me – as a *friend*! We're talking detachments, *battalions*, of blokes who like me as a friend and screw those tarts they supposedly hate.

Hold it here. I have to stop here, to state as an author that my sexual contribution to society is an embarrassment. A miserable non-contribution, that's what it is. I mean, I've screwed two guys. That's it, and some screws they were!

Birdy was my first.

I asked him one day, as a friend:

"Birdy, how d'you feel about fucking me? Would you do it?"

"No way, Bulika." (That's what my two close buddies call me – short for bullterrier. Fucking arseholes. I'll give them a fucking bullterrier!) "We're friends."

"Fine," I said. "We'll stay friends. But do it to me, just once, so at least I know what it's like!"

He accepted. Took me to his place. Took off his clothes, folded the sheet and threw it down to the floor.

"Lie down."

"I like big tits," he said, making me feel all warm and fuzzy inside. I mean, I do have big tits, and I'm all happy he got a hard-on. I guess I'm no throwaway. All you have to do is approach the guy in a friendly way.

As soon as we finished, he got dressed. When I came back from the bathroom, he was already at the door:

"I'm just gonna throw this sheet into the trash so Goca doesn't smell the blood. I'll be right back."

Goca – that's Birdy's fiancée and, supposedly, my friend.

Dick Gruja was my second. I did it several times with him.

At the summer camp in Povile, fucking was the main recreational activity. You know – sun, sand, moonlight – the bonking Grand Slam. I mean, you'd slip on a used condom more often than on a melon rind, though it was the season for both – melons and fucking. With me, however – sweet f.a. Nobody asked. Or I didn't know how to offer, I'm not sure.

It's true that the business manager of the camp – Dick Gruja – had an eye on me, but I wasn't going to do it with him for a lifetime of guaranteed screwing! No way! So I told him to piss off every time he came on to me. Still, he didn't give up.

Then, one day, I asked him to give me a ride in his truck to Baške Vode, where he goes shopping.

"No problem. Except that I charge for the ride in natural currency."

"Fine," I said.

I'm thinking – this better be a joke. I mean, shit, the guy's fifty! And not only that. Strong, knobbly legs. Always barefooted. Hairy. Bald. In short, he looked like a dick – with the bald head as HEAD, if you can picture it. So since his real name was Gruja, I called him Dick Gruja.

So on the way back from Baške Vode, Dick Gruja simply makes a turn off the highway on to the dirt road towards the woods. He stops the truck in some kind of underbrush. "Time to pay for the ride, baby," he says, lifting my skirt. I'm kicking and screaming as much as I can, but we're smack in the middle of nowhere and the jerk surprised me, you know, embarrassed me. He could have been my father, man! Twice over, no less. So anyway, he takes out his dick and wants to stick it in my mouth. I push him back. He doesn't let go. I screech. He grabs my legs.

We wrestled for a while there until at the end, we ended up fucking on the seat. I gave up. Had me fucking covered in bruises. Bit my tits off too.

"So, your arm didn't fall off after all, eh? You liked it, eh?" he rattles on our way back to the camp.

"Why d'you fuckin' bite my tits like that? Are you nuts? You demented moron!"

"I've never tasted better ones, I swear!"

I have to admit, I was glad about the tits.

We did it a few more times. In the warehouse, on flattened cardboard boxes. We did everything. The only thing I refused to do was give him a blow-job. I mean, he has four kids! Two of them older than me. But the sea, the moonlight, tralala, I couldn't resist. I knew I would be pissed off with myself after, but I kept going back and getting laid on those damn cardboard boxes.

He called me once or twice even when I went back to Belgrade, but I said no thank you. Too embarrassing.

That's it. Not much for a gel of twenty-two. I don't seem to meet the current standard. Big tits aren't in. Neither is my big gob. I guess I'm a little too much for our macho-patriarchal guys. Even Bonehead sometimes says: "Shut your trap", when he gets fed up with my incessant blaguing.

Bla bla. Why am I telling you all this? Well, I've got some explaining to do. For a while now, I've been "entertaining the idea" of getting Bonehead into bed, but I just haven't had the balls to do anything about it. I'm thinking – I just don't turn him on. Besides, it's not like he would be the only guy to "like me as a friend". Also, the idea of bringing a wounded soldier to your home and proceeding to sexually exploit him sounds a little too French, a little too twisted for my taste. So anyway, I lie in my bed for days and days and just wait. Sometimes, he roams around the house at night. I activate my radar. Solid hard-on, fifteen feet northwest. Yeah, I wish – he goes right back to bed. So I dream about him. In the dream, I'm even giving him a blow-job, but I'm mostly just kissing him all over his clean, white skin. And his dark hair. Thick, shiny, like the mane of a stallion.

Does this explain the "sigh of relief"? You bet it does.

So anyway, he sticks his hand in my bosom and he gets into this heavy-duty kneading action. I can't help but wonder if it's my grandma and grandpa/uncle's screwing confession that got him all hot and steamy. I mean, who on this planet, other than my grandmother would make anyone want to do it with me?! I let him knead the dough a while longer, to really turn him on. The guy could change his mind any minute, being a Bonehead. So I keep reading, like it's just not doing anything for my erotic appetite:

It seemed to me that Jelena was taking great caution to hide something about her relationship with the barbarian.

* * *

By now, he's stuck his other hand in and he keeps squeezin' and a' rubbin'. I'm still reading:

It is possible that something insignificant is in question. My last hope, a hypothesis I have been testing for days with rather inconclusive results, is that she is hiding something in order to protect me from certain unsettling discoveries. But what discoveries? Unfortunately, I was aware that this hypothesis, however convenient, wasn't probable. The certainty which I faced was the dilution of Jelena's disgust towards the Communist barbarian and her agreement to write Stavra's biography for one of the very worst amongst them . . .

Here, I just couldn't hold my breath anymore. I threw the manuscript to the ground, catapulted from the armchair and reached for Bonehead's fly. I grabbed his manhood. What beauty! I shoved it in my mouth. It all felt like in my dreams, but much more intense.

We kept going at it till 5 a.m. – the last time in morning light. What can I say – Bonehead is a god. Bonehead rules!

V

When I asked Bonehead to make an inventory of all the papers from the bag in Scumbag's closet, he was all for it. You see, us two fact-investigating and novel-assembling adventurists have to have an idea of what's at our disposal. We've got to have something straightforward, in black and white, to put all of Grandma's odds and ends into some kind of life perspective, you know? Life trinkets in a canvas bag.

So in his leisurely hours of convalescence, not only did my sweet Bonehead compose an inventory, not only did he type up three crisp copies, but he also came up with an elegant new title for the canvas bag! Imagine that! He worked until the cows came home and one day, he emerged from a room saying:

"Jela, I finished the INVENTARIUM HELENAE."

My little straight-A Latin pussy cat. I kissed him on the forehead.

We examined the material at our disposal.

"There'll be some gaps," he said.

"Slow down. We haven't collected everything yet. Not everything is in the Inventarium. We have Kojović, we have the archives, another witness might come along . . ." I blabbed on but I basically felt the same way – there'll be major gaps! I mean, who's heard of making a story without gaps out of a bagful of fifty-year-old papers? I concluded my presentation:

"If there are gaps, so be it. Right, Bonehead?"

"Sure. But we shouldn't kill ourselves over it, should we?"

"I like your title very much."

"See? And you didn't believe me when I told you classical languages always come in handy."

And here it is, items 1 to 31, accompanied by our insightful comments:

INVENTARIUM HELENAE

1. Seminar presentation for prof. Dr Vladeta Popović – Jelena Ljubisavljević: "The Black Lady in Shakespeare's Sonnets".

2. Seminar presentation paper in English – Jelena Ljubisavljević: "Alexander Pope at Binfield – 'The Rape of the Lock' and 'Windsor Forest'".

3. Translation of the short story "Red" by Somerset Maugham.*

4. Translation of the essay "La Gioconda" by Walter Pater.

5. Translation of the poem "I Dream'd in a Dream" by Walt Whitman.

6. Translation of the poem "Daffodils" by William Wordsworth.

7. Translation of the poem "Ode to a Nightingale" by John Keats (first five stanzas only).

8. Translation of the poem "Soul's Beauty" by Dante Gabriel Rossetti.

9. Translation of the poem "The Hour Before Dawn" by William Butler Yeats.

10. Translation of the poem "Annabel Lee" by Edgar Allan Poe.

11. Translation of the poems "Clair de lune" and "Chansons d'automne" by Paul Verlaine.

12. Translation of the poem "Bateau ivre" by Arthur Rimbaud.

13. Translation of the poem "L'après-midi d'un faune" by Stéphane Mallarmé.

14. "The Jabberwocky Variations" – a dubious prose charade most likely written by Granny Jelena. It's almost impossible to synopsize and I'm sure it's not worth publishing at all. It's not even signed and it basically tells us exactly nil about Grandma's life.

* After every translation, at the end, in parentheses, it says the same thing: Translated by Jelena Ljubisavljević-Arandjelović.

15. *"My anguished and wretched treatise"* – what else do I call it? Falls under Fiction. Twenty-six single-spaced pages of Jovan's shall we say – confession. The reader has thus far read two excerpts of this piece of literary gold. The third excerpt will be featured soon.

16. Twenty-four letters, of which twenty-three are addressed to Jelena, written by Jovan, while one is Jelena's letter to Jovan. The latter was never mailed. The letters addressed to Jelena are mostly insignificant, except for one – Krsman's – which, frankly, is a total puzzle. However, the *letter addressed to Jovan (unmailed)* and *Krsman's letter addressed to Jelena (unclear)*, are pretty significant so we'll find room for them in the book later on, for the purposes of "progressing the action" as dear old Archer would say. Maybe it's worth mentioning, though definitely not printing, yet another letter, the one written to Jelena by Siniša Ristić and mailed from Vrnjačka Banja. It should suffice to notify the reader that Jovan's evaluation of this fellow ("a good-looking, slickly combed nitwit with a tandem") was not yellow-green with jealousy, but accurate: Siniša was a total moron for sure (that's the guy who kissed my grandma at the gate, if my grandpa/uncle's account is to be trusted).

17. Birth certificate of Jelena Ljubisavljević from "The Book of the Born and Deceased" of the Serbian Orthodox Church at the Temple of the Resurrection in Belgrade for the year 1923.

18. Half of a pre-war 100-dinar bill.

19. The brochure "London Programme for Overseas Students – Summer Term 1937".

20. Train ticket for the London Underground (First Class, June 17th 1937).

21. Ticket from London's Old Vic theatre (December 6th 1936).

22. A lock of hair in a green envelope – no date or caption.

23. Insurance Identification Card – the "Group Insurance Programme", issued in 1937, in London, to the name of Jelena Ljubisavljević.

24. A 1937 letter from "Société Internationale des Chemins de Fer Français" in which Le Chef du Bureau Principal – Gare de Paris-Lyon-Bercy – informs Mademoiselle Jelena Ljubisavljević that the lost parcel with books had not been found and that "les recherches entreprises sont demeurées unfructueuses".

25. A letter of similar content from "Schweitz Zolamt – Bureau des Douanes Suisses".

26. A National Library membership card from 1941.

27. A certificate of merit given to Jelena Ljubisavljević dated July 12th 1942, subtitled "Everything for Serbia, Nothing against it: Only Unity saves the Serbs" – for collecting relief for Serbian war prisoners in Germany.

28. A certificate in which the "City Authorities of Belgrade certifies that Jelena Ljubisavljević, born to father Socrates Ljubisavljević and mother Olivera Ljubisavljević-born Nerandžić", had officially added the surname Arandjelović to hers, and that she would henceforth use the name Jelena Ljubisavljević-Arandjelović in all official documents.

29. *The front pages of the daily "Politika" dated 27th and 28th of November 1944* with the names of executed citizens and an editorial by a fucking leftist demagogue by the name of Marko Ristić, commenting on the executions of 105 traitors under the title "A collective death for those who collectively embraced war crimes".

30. *The Biography of Stavra Arandjelović*, as written by my dear granny, and already presented in the third chapter.

31. Photographs. Since my pal and publisher is on his way to making gobs of money (some coffee shop owner expressed an interest in sponsoring the book), maybe we'll stick some of these guys in.

We've italicised the items we're gonna put in as well as those you've already seen.

I'd like to add one more thing:

For purposes of visual and aesthetic harmony, and to lend a note of credibility to the Inventarium, here is the front page of the "Politika", dated November 28 1944, found in Jelena's bag.

Since the script is ridiculously tiny, some of you will be too lazy to bother with Marko's leftist spiel, so that's why I'm copying the end of his editorial. 'Twould be a pity to miss it:

". . . Those responsible for this massive crime were the ones who issued orders and Germany's servants – Nedić himself, Ljotić himself, Draža Mihailović himself. Though mere servants to the occupier, they also issued orders (*So what the fuck were they – servants or command-givers? – comment – Bonehead and I*), their orders paralleled Germany's, since their strivings paralleled Germany's: Both strived for the destruction of the people's source of strength and identity, indeed of anything which might have obstructed their goal to reign, exploit, plunder and dominate. The third, equally responsible group of traitors are the intermediaries, who were the messengers of the orders. The executors, who shot, slaughtered, denounced and tortured were simultaneously the instrument of the German oppressor and of those who ruled before them, who remained in power under the Germans and who hoped they would stay there after the Germans.

It is in the light of that knowledge that one must read the declaration of the Court Martial of the First Corpus of the People's Liberational Army of Yugoslavia. Those who collectively embraced crime, collectively embraced death: Nedić's ministers and agents of the special police, district chiefs and denouncers, members of the Court Martial of Serbia's State Guard and Pećanac's Chetniks,* generals and agents of the Gestapo, university professors and police officers, bearers of the Karadjordje Star and Draza's slaughterers . . . (*So what do you think – is it really equally disgraceful to be a bearer of the Karadjordje Star, an agent of the Special Police, a university prof and a Gestapo general? We got some messed up notions of right and wrong here – one more comment from Bonehead and me.*)

It so happens that amongst the slaughterers and agents, amongst that scum of traitors and war criminals, are also those whom

* Kosta Pećanac: Chetnik commander who operated independently of the Chetnik commander Draža Mihailović. Pećanac Chetniks occasionally collaborated with the Germans in their struggle against the Communist Partisans.

Belgrade until recently considered its respectable citizens. These traitors, imposing themselves as the elite of Serbia, are a disgrace to this people, but their deaths are not. The face of this people has been saved; its glory is a deserved one. As for those who betrayed their people, who in this portentous and crucial conflict joined forces with the foreign invader in a war against their own people, their extermination has already begun. (*So those 105 were really just a moderate beginning. The shit had yet to come! – our third and last comment*). The stain of betrayal is far too superficial to leave a trace on the face of this people. With the unerring hand of justice, we shall wash that stain away forever, our faces beaming victoriously.

Marko Ristić"

Thou art in deep shit, oh ye countries with a Marko Ristić for moral judge. (My comment.)

VI

We almost stood Kojović up.

I'd telephoned the old man that morning. I said to him:

"Reads like a novel in parts, Mr Kojović."

The old guy went nuts over this. I went on:

"Your gift with words, Mr Kojović, matches Roger Martin du Gard's, I swear to God. Shame we called it quits just as it was getting interesting. Male sex kitten captivates attention of female sex kitten."

"To be continued, to be continued, Miss Jelena. However, I will take the liberty of suggesting a different meeting place. It was much too noisy at Kandinsky's place. In fact, it would be a great pleasure if you came to my flat tonight. We could continue our conversation in peace, and you would also witness something else: the old doctor of philosophy making spaghetti à la bolognese as if he'd been brought up on nothing but pasta."

Mr Bilogorac is also invited, providing I find that suitable. Yes, I do find Mr Bilogorac suitable, as well as Kojović's suggestion to come after 9 p.m., when it's cooler, since his top-floor studio (where he's been living on a "temporary" basis for the last half-century) gets sweltering in the daytime.

Okey-pokey.

Around eight, we passed by the Bermuda Triangle (which is on the way since the old man lives on Jevremova Street) to see what's new with the "gentlemen students", as Old Fiacre so graciously calls them ("gentleman student" – that's more or less like saying "Gipsy Baron"). We had absolutely no idea that the student strikers had in the meantime organized a protest walk through the centre of Belgrade. So Bonehead and I roamed around the philosophy department for a while, listened to a few smart arses in the amphitheatre of the philology department, talked politics with a couple of fourth-year drama stooges, when suddenly, one gentleman student from the "sapient" leadership – the cross-eyed one, whatsisname, his picture's in the paper – one of the head strikers, anyway, he saw that Bonehead was on crutches.

"Excuse me, are you a student at this department?" he asked Bonehead. Bonehead said "Nope", he's from Osijek. Here our cross-eyed friend squeaked with inner joy, went completely delirious over Bonehead.

"Are you wounded, Bogdan?" he asked. Bonehead, horror-stricken, looked over to see if I was going to jump to his rescue. Since I merely shrugged my shoulders, he admitted that yes, he had been wounded a month ago at Turshan's Hill near Teochak, by a grenade. Even less would have provoked an acute onset of diarrhoea in whatsisname: the students are against the war, but not against the victims of the war, heroism is heroism, the blokes defending Moslavina are not at fault – the ones who've pushed them into this mess are, i.e. – Sloba, Karadžić, Kertes and company . . . . life, death, the aftermath, tralala, and the next thing you know – Bonehead, his crutches and I are in the front-line of the fucking demonstration, taking a "slow and dignified walk" through central Belgrade.

"Tell them your leg hurts," I advise in my well-practised stage whisper.

"My leg hurts," he says.

No problem they say, wait till we get around the corner, we'll take a picture for the paper and then you can slip out of the line.

Yeah, of course! We went all the way around again before getting away from them.

Sweaty and breathless ("lift out of order") we finally made it to Kojović's third-floor studio. It was after ten-thirty.

"Sorry," I explain, "the revolution."

The old sweetie-pie isn't upset. The water for the pasta is boiling but first we must taste his apricot brandy. Are we in the mood for some apricot brandy from his native town of Klenak?

You bet we are.

I don't remember how we got talking about Scumbag.

Actually, I do.

I remember:

Kojović asked why I call Mr Bilogorac "Bonehead":

I'd prepared my answer:

"Because Mr Bilogorac *is* a Bonehead."

"But Miss Jelena! Such words!"

I explained everything:

"A patriot, left nearly legless, who can't wait to go and get showered with bullets in Moslavina again, who studies Geodesy, tolerates me and thinks that all humans are innately good except Croatians, which he calls a breed of cockroaches resistant to chemical weapons, cannot by nature be anything but a Bonehead. Need I say more?"

"I ain't from Moslavina, I'm from Grubišno Polje, and I ain't studying Geodesy but Geography though my thesis has to do with Geodesy – determining the coordinates of points on Earth through astronomic observation. Don't listen to her, Mr Doctor, Jelena just likes to joke around."

And then the nutcase proceeded to defend me:

"You know what they say – Dirty mouth, golden heart . . ."

Bladi bla. He would have gone on, I swear, if I hadn't intervened:

"I have a dirty mouth and a big arse, as for big hearts, they tend to be the property of Boneheads from Moslavina."

He wasn't angry, of course. Bonehead can tolerate everything with a smile and a good-natured "Go to hell, Jela. You're always mucking 'round." The only thing he doesn't like, he tells Kojović:

"I don't like hearing her call her mother – Scumbag."

That's how we got on to Scumbag.

"That's . . . Lena's daughter? I saw her as a baby, at the Nerandžićs'," the poor man replied tentatively, just for the sake of saying something. He was shitting himself; he had no idea what kind of response he might get from me. The old bloke thinks I'm cool, mostly, from what I see, but he sort of looks at me like I'm some kind of exotic anaconda from the tropical bush of Ceylon: I'm colourful, large, and it's not clear if I am dangerous when I'm hungry.

"Yes," I said, "Scumbag is the daughter of your friend Lena."

"*Ignoscas saepe alteri, numquam tibi,*" he said.

"What does it mean?" I asked.

Bonehead's quick on the draw:

"Forgive much to thy neighbour, little to thyself."

"You don't have a good relationship with your mother?" Kojović continued with caution.

"We don't have a relationship. Scumbag is . . . hey, Bonehead, how far is Scumbag from the homeland? In kilometres, that is?"

"From Zagreb to New Zealand?"

"Yeah. From Zagreb to New Zealand."

"By air?"

"And how else?"

"By boat."

"With Yugoslav Airlines, you bozo, with JAT!"

"It don't fly anymore."

"Give me the answer, or I'll break your other leg."

Bonehead's laughing his head off. Teasing. Finally, he says:

"Oh, around 15,000 kilometres, I'd say."

"Then, Scumbag is about 16,000 kilometres away from Belgrade, Mr Kojović."

"There ain't 1,000 kilometres between Belgrade and Zagreb," our pedantic astronomic geodesist replied.

"Yes there are," I said, "via Budapest and Reykjavik – which is the route all normal blockaded Serbs prefer to the short one."

Kojović is curious to know what Scumbag is doing in New Zealand:

"Is your mother there on business or . . . ."

"Nope. She got married. Five years ago. The Maori bloke wanted her, but he didn't want the luggage. So Scumbag grabbed his hand and left me at the airport as excess baggage. It's not her fault that I weighed more than sixty pounds even five years ago."

"Who took care of you after her departure?" Kojović asks, "Your father?"

"Well, sort of. The poor guy doesn't exactly have an easy time of it – he's a chemist, married to a bimbo, two little kids, works part-time as a prof, can't get enough classes to be full-time, while his life companion wastes the quids away on her lipstick and mascara collection. He'd help me out but he doesn't have enough. Scumbag used to send me $250 a month, regularly, until this blockade came through. He does help me out, occasionally, when he has extra. What the hell am I talking about!? Fuck'em!" (My love and forgiveness act could hold no longer.) "Both can go to hell. Such unbelievable arseholes, both of them! When Santa Claus was distributing parents, at least he could have dropped off one in working condition under my tree."

Kojović was about to say something, but I couldn't shut up:

"Bla bla. Enough of that – we came here to listen and not to rabbit on. I sound like I studied Rhetoric at the Sremski Karlovci Gymnasium! OK, here we go: 'The love-life of Grandma Jelena – part two'. Shall we, Mr Kojović?"

"We shall, we shall. Let me just throw the spaghetti into the pot."

Fantastic spaghetti. Real parmigiano, home-grated by Kojović himself. Oregano. The old geezer must've been Italian in his previous incarnation.

So, here we are. Pasta, a bottle of rosé, the works. The tape recorder clicks away, the old man twitters on. The book writes itself:

OLD MAN KOJOVIĆ (2)

OLD FIACRE:

Where did we leave off, Miss Jelena?

ME:

Jelena The First asked the gipsy major to see about Stavra.

OLD FIACRE:

Yes, and to my enormous surprise, she didn't just ask – she pleaded. Her plea sounded a little bit like an order, but it was a plea nonetheless. But I was wrong last time: she was no longer pleading with a major; Krsman Jakšić had been promoted to the rank of lieutenant colonel. Hence, she asked Lieutenant Colonel Jakšić: "Lieutenant Colonel, could you please find out where my stepfather Stavra Arandjelović is and when he will face trial?" That was how she said it. I remember now.

At that moment, my dear young friends, though startled beyond measure by Jelena's question, I was still composed enough to consider what the crafty rascal might reply. Indeed, I was sure that even if he knew something about Stavra, Krsman would pretend he had never heard of him. At best. In the worst and more likely case scenario, he would criticize Jelena for inquiring about that collaborationist, capitalist, treasonist and whatever other sort of vermin.

The Communist language is worth analysing, you see. It's a most gratifying project, believe me. Their language gives them away. It is sombre, graceless, and savage insults are its only norm. Yet, Krsman did not resort to such words! I was startled for the second time in only a few seconds. Krsman selected softer words, words virtually unknown in his dialect, and responded in a flash, as if he'd been waiting for Jelena's question. That was my impression at the time, at least.

Let there be no confusion about it – Krsman was too much of a Communist not to pronounce, on such an occasion, a certain few mandatory phrases from their catechism: "Stavra will not face a corrupt Capitalist court. He will face the People's Court, who will justly separate the chaff from the grain. Citizen Stavra has nothing to fear if he is innocent."

Mind you, dear children, plenty of innocent heads were rolling down streets all over Yugoslavia in those days! More than in Turkish times, even! The more heads are hurled down the wasteland, the louder the Krsmans of this world get about the justice of the People's Court! Such blasphemy! The end of language, the wreckage of words, I tell you, my young friends. A veritable killer virus, that is what Communist jargon was.

Hearing their grave and self-righteous proclamations, I often asked myself: "Where is their presence of mind, how can they utter such gruesome obscenities!" It was harder for me to grasp their hypocrisy than their brutality, you see. Hypocrisy perhaps isn't the correct term for it. I never managed to determine whether they were lying shamelessly to us as well as to themselves when uttering their inviolable propaganda claptrap, or whether, blinded by vengeful lust, they really believed in such obvious lies, as long as the lies confirmed their divine Communist omniscience. You mentioned that you have at home the "Politika" front page with Ristić's editorial and the list of those 105 executed "war criminals". Well, I personally knew at least ten individuals from that list, whose only war crime was that they worked as actors, clerks, professors, journalists in Nedić's Serbia. Can you imagine how we read that front page when it came out? Miss Jelena? Mr Bilogorac? The whole front page and part of the second, crawling with names and two-line descriptions of the acts of treason supposedly deserving death by firing squad! Let us skip exclusions, punishments, prison terms and save time by going straight to executions! And that according to the rightful, people's decision of the Court Martial!

Still, the People's Court is unerring, Krsman says without a blink. The chaff from the grain, thank you very much! Perhaps – I say that because I truly do not know – perhaps the lie about the just People's Court was the holiest of holy truths as far as Krsman was concerned. Naturally, regardless of what the Krsmans of this world believed, the court was not just, but in Krsman's mouth, that nontruth had a different chemical composition from the lies of, say, Marko Ristić, who knew that he was lying out of greed. Krsman, it seems, didn't know that. Krsman was a murderer. Marko Ristić a liar. You see, that is what I'd like to explain to you, though I'm afraid you can't fully comprehend it.

BONEHEAD:

'Course we can.

ME:

We can. They still lie today. They lie like children.

OLD FIACRE:

Yes of course, they lie as you said, like children, politicians always do, because they are manipulating a crowd with a childlike capacity for reasoning. But there is something else I wish to point out to you. You see, Communists believed that "class hatred" was a noble emotion, such as "motherly love", for instance, something unquestionable. I think that Krsman didn't lie the way politicians did, that Krsman and his sort lived in a trance which made them clinically blind and deaf, at least for a while, to the injustices they were committing in the name of their brand of justice. It is a sort of disorder, you see – like the epileptic seizures of Partisan veterans at their massive gatherings. The epiphenomenons of the wild Communist phenomenon.

I have to change gear here. Kojović's gone a little too far in the direction of the irrelevant. I act with the intention of returning him, as the structuralists would say (and they get all pumped up when they say it – they think they've got God by the balls or something!) into the *Narrative Plane*.

ME:

So what we have is – the lieutenant colonel is preaching to the beautiful Jelena from the Communist Iliad.

Kojović freaked. He started complimenting me. "The Beautiful Jelena from the Communist Iliad"! Ah, brilliantly stated! Meanwhile, my ears are red with pain, my embarrassment is growing by the second and the old freak thinks I'm marketing myself as a literary writer! Bonehead joins the mess:

BONEHEAD:

I tell you – when Jela rattles off something nutty, nobody does it better.

In the name of saving my own life, I urgently needed to say something normal:

ME:

All right, enough literary jawing on. Mr Kojović, I've got a question: How come Jelena listened to Krsman's spiel about the just court without saying a word?

OLD FIACRE:

Well, you see, Miss Jelena, it wasn't exactly a spiel. If by spiel you mean – sermon. It was a sermon in passing, but in essence, Krsman actually gave a firm promise that he would investigate, do everything he could and so on – providing he is convinced that Stavra is innocent.

"I told you that Stavra is innocent". Even today, Jelena's sentence resonates in my mind. Her words sounded so icy, threatening, relentless, that Krsman immediately curtailed his lecturing and complied.

One must know that the Serbian peasant (and Krsman was a peasant, both before and after he had been promoted to the rank of lieutenant colonel) is first and foremost – a finagler: an untrustworthy, congenital blasphemer. Nothing is sacred to the likes of him. That was Krsman's nature exactly. I remember, for example, once we were listening to Beethoven's Fifth on Tanjug's record player. An Englishman, a Radio London correspondent, had brought the record to us. "What you got there?" Krsman asked. "Beethoven's Fifth Symphony," I said. "Oh yeah? And who says it ain't the fourth one?" replied the guffawing Krsman. "Oh yeah-and-who-says" was a common expression in his vocabulary and I believe that it reflects the condition of the Serbian peasant spirit better than any other. That is why I think that somewhere deep in the foundations of Krsman's faith, there was a genetic, sceptical crack. The "Oh-yeah-and-who-says" crack would completely destroy the Communist morale in a year or two, though even at the time, at its paradisiac inception, it was beginning to generate internal quakes irreconcilable with the unadulterated dogmatism and bigotry of the early days.

The Serbian finagler, you see, simply cannot be a dogmatist. Krsman was shrewd, cunning, and he realized soon enough that Stavra was the direct road to Jelena. He wouldn't have missed that opportunity for the world. That is how I perceive Krsman's softness. I think that my speculations were correct: that moment was also the beginning of Jelena's softening and – however unlikely it seemed at the time – the growing intimacy between Krsman and her.

The old fellow makes a little rhetorical pause. He's thinking. I let him think. I guess that's how he was taught at the Karlovci Gymnasium in the BC era.

"You see, Miss Jelena," he says, with his index finger pointing upward, "between our first encounter and now, I had time to establish what I truly know about the further rapport between Krsman and the beautiful Jelena from the Communist Iliad. I began by relating my memories and leaving the gap-filling and conclusions to you. Sadly, from the onset of the collaboration between Jelena and Krsman, those gaps, away from my field of vision at the time, grow bigger and bigger. You see, more and more often, Krsman would ask Jelena to step out of the room whenever he had something to communicate to her. They would stand on the spiral iron staircase, the shortest route from the printing department to our floor, talking in whispers. If anyone appeared, they'd stop their conversation. They would resume only when the person fell out of earshot. Jelena with her arms folded on her chest, leaning slightly against the railing, shoulders slightly pulled back and hips thrown slightly forward; Krsman leaning against the railing with one arm, hovering above Jelena like a mighty dark cloud. He – tall as a mountain and she – tiny as a small, priceless porcelain bird from the Sung dynasty. They looked truly incongruous and unreal together – the product of a sick imagination with a penchant for arbitrary pictorial and social transpositions."

The old fart is a drearier juggler than Jacques from the "Circus Internazional", I'm thinking to myself. "The product of a sick imagination with a penchant for arbitrary pictorial and social transpositions!" Kojović is mixing words like a mad alchemist.

Anyway, going on:

OLD FIACRE:

As you can see, I am sidestepping the narrative rule of only relating what I saw and heard, otherwise I wouldn't have much to relate. I sidestep it with pleasure, as consistency is not a quality I particularly respect. Consistency, my dear young friends, is the hallway leading to all dogmatism . . .

ME:

Right, Mr Kojović. Be as inconsistent as you possibly can! So let's get to those assumptions.

OLD FIACRE:

I don't have any choice, Miss Jelena. Krsman and my beautiful young colleague now had a secret, and Jelena wasn't expressing any interest in sharing the least part of that secret with me. Once or twice, my curiosity led me to try to find something out about the attempt to save my dear friend Mr Stavra, but Jelena evidently avoided filling me in on the progress of things. She would answer my questions vaguely and unwillingly, hinting that my curiosity was inappropriate. The secret which Jelena and Krsman shared, nurtured and developed in their dealings and schemings, murmurings and mutterings, created a conspiratorial kind of intimacy between them. They communicated with stares and glances, received and dispatched wordless messages, spoke in codes, knew something others didn't know – in short, they were hiding something which made them partners. And conspiratorial intimacy between two people, particularly if they are a man and a woman (often lovers), cannot be concealed. Certainly, the Jelena whom I knew so thoroughly couldn't conceal it from me. Observing them day in day out, pretending to be slow-witted and blind to their consultations and deliberations, I quickly began suspecting that freeing Stavra was not the only secret shared by these two shockingly different creatures.

For a few days now, in preparation for this conversation of ours, I have been searching for the exact words to describe the new element in Jelena's expression, in the tone of her voice when addressing Krsman, in her gaze, in the way she lowered her eyes whenever she felt I had discovered in them something that was not supposed to be open to discovery. I have searched in vain, for I didn't find the right words. It's no wonder that I didn't. Their type of secret communication is resistant to verbal description because it is done with signs finer than language, signals more radiant than communicative: it is the tremor of bodies rather than the motion of minds. Cobwebs, the finest, softest, most delicate cobwebs, virtually invisible, shrouding words, movements and glances – that is what comes to mind. You know the cobweb is there only when it delicately tickles you around the eyes and instantly disappears, leaving you to wonder if you've actually felt anything or if sleepiness is making you imagine things.

So there you are, Miss Jelena. I have no evidence whatsoever, I cannot point my finger in any specific direction, nor support my sentiment that the iron stairwell and office encounters between Jelena and Krsman were not their only encounters. I had no basis for thinking so but I would have sworn that my suspicions were accurate: something preceded their public encounters and something else, safe from the glare of the world around them, followed.

BONEHEAD:

So then, they did, didn't they?

ME:

Did what?

BONEHEAD:

I mean . . . fall in love . . . with each other.

ME:

What's the matter with you? You cheering for the gipsy now?

OLD FIACRE:

I wouldn't go that far with my conclusions, Mr Bilogorac. Neither then, nor now. My insolent guesswork ended with the conviction that their meetings extended beyond working hours. Small remarks, very rare careless slips revealed that: for instance, Jelena would say "What I gave you yesterday . . . ", when I knew that they hadn't seen each other yesterday in Tanjug. I don't quite recall all the details of this type which gave them away, but there were enough of them for the conclusion I had reached.

ME:

Still, I mean – was there coitus or what?

OLD FIACRE:

It doesn't seem probable. Try as I may, I cannot imagine Jelena – all foam, white skin and smooth black hair, my dear poor Lena, teeming with futile scorn, heroic sarcasm and deep, though inadequately concealed inner pain; a Lena dressed in virginally starched clothing, forbidden bourgeois lace and silk stockings – I cannot picture the white Jelena from Senjak in the embrace of a baker named Krsman who killed a thousand men and slept with a thousand women! And that which I cannot imagine, my dear children, I cannot believe!

I believe that Jelena perceived herself as a Christian martyr sacrificing herself for the salvation of her stepfather: a Belgrade Judith saving Bethulia from Holofernes' siege and the pestilence of the Assyrians. Naturally, as I've already told you, it was only guesswork. I didn't know. I wasn't sure, but as I watched her, I saw a great deal.

87

I saw, for example, that the superior-inferior arrangement between Jelena and Krsman in essence did not change. Jelena was still the sovereign, the magistrate, still the one distributing rewards and assigning punishments, though with less, significantly less cruelty than before. Krsman was still the one who listened, made the effort to speak with a Belgrade accent and not to swear, though with a new sort of mindset. It was a mere nuance, you know, but quite a significant one. Before, Krsman had no self-confidence to speak of in front of Jelena, and he pretended otherwise. Now, he had gained the self-confidence, but he was shrewdly concealing it, rightfully fearing that it could anger his strict sovereign. With time, however, Krsman's self-confidence grew more, as did Jelena's leniency. The astute eye, the eye well trained in the art of observing Senjak's Judith, hence – my own eye, could not miss the incessantly spreading cavity in Jelena's hitherto enormous, nearly disagreeable arrogance. In her arrogance, which was solid and unyielding as a diamond before the hatching of the conspiracy, I started detecting clear signs of static instability, a new, hitherto unknown form of nervousness, something akin to fear, hesitation. It was a kind of disharmony, but a disharmony so pale, so well controlled from the inside, that I never dared draw any conclusions about its nature. I barely perceived it, and it never struck me, neither then nor now, that one could easily dissect it and explain it.

ME:

I'll bet you a million: She fell for him – my granny fell for some baker and part-time goat-herder! I bet she did!

OLD FIACRE:

I accept the bet, and I say that she didn't! No question about it! Jelena was simply making compromises with the savage masters of this country, the masters of life and death; she was doing everything within her power to save the life of her stepfather. Her compromise might have gone far or stopped at very small concessions, but there was no question of love. I know Jelena. I know her stubbornness. Her decisiveness. She was a fragile beauty and a fierce fighter. She was simply going to save Stavra – and when Jelena heads off somewhere, I know this from the time she was first learning to walk – straight is her pathway. There is no winding around, no shortcuts. *Ad augusta per angusta.* Stavra's head lay on the block – the axe needed to be stopped. Imagine your father being sentenced to death by firing squad . . .

ME:

My chemist – to the firing squad?! Hey, nobody messes with my chemist!

OLD FIACRE:

Stavra Arandjelović was a man worth saving, and Jelena a person incapable of surrendering, a person who follows her sense of duty to the end, like a Spanish doña from the time of the Saracens.

ME:

OK, then tell me this much: was Stavra really doing dirty deeds with the Nazis or did they top him just for the fun of it?

The old fellow isn't answering quite yet. I know we're on to something hot, but I can't tell if he's glad I'm picking away at this stuff, or what. He takes a sip of wine. Frowns. Classic thinking mode. This goes on for a while, so Bonehead decides to interject:

BONEHEAD:

I don't think it would happen just like that. I mean, our people were also killing, but only the really evil fellers – the Ustaše.* With the Domobrans,† they would just smack 'em a few times and send them to labour camps.

ME:

Yeah right. And you remember it all quite well.

BONEHEAD:

Well, no, I don't. Of course not. But my grandpa told me stories. And everybody else too. Everyone knew. It was common knowledge.

OLD FIACRE:

Well, it was and it wasn't, Mr Bilogorac. Until very recently – yesterday practically, talking about the crimes and punishments of those tempestuous years was impossible. It isn't possible today, but for

* Croatian military group notorious for persecuting Serbs, Jews and Gipsies; 1941–45.
† Regular army of the Nazi-affiliated Independent State of Croatia; 1941–45.

opposite reasons. Yesterday's criminals become today's saints and the saints transform into betailed satans. The Communists have been driving their constricted, victor's truth into people's heads for too long. Under such circumstances and the pressure of the many elapsed decades, the simple truth becomes disfigured, unrecognizable and forever unestablishable. Stavra's destiny best exemplifies that.

Was Stavra Arandjelović guilty, you ask? What can I tell you? From the Communist angle of viewing things – he was. From the patriotic – not at all. Stavra despised the Communists the way a peasant who acquired everything he has with God's help and hard labour from morning to night, must despise plunderers, idlers and thieves. Communists were destroyers and desecrators; Stavra was a builder, preserver. He perceived power in the hands of the landless idlers and pettifoggers as an unjust punishment from God.

I remember having a conversation with him sometime around the autumn of 1942. We had run into each other at Kalimegdan Park and took a slow stroll to his house in Krunska Street. We both carried in our pockets the last issue of *The Serbian People* and were discussing a column by Velmar-Janković titled "He who is a Communist is not a Serb". Stavra was confirming Velmar-Janković's argument that the Serbs had always been heroes and patriots, but never Inter-nationalists and Communists. He was also fond of Velmar-Janković's idea that among us, the homespun man ruled, and not the crook. However, it was with disgust and contempt that he referred to the blasphemous statement by Jonić's deputy that we should emulate the German Reich in everything and that the Reich was ardently assisting us in the renewal of our race, our culture and our education! "Assisting us" – I remember Stavra's exasperated words – "by oppressing us! How can there be so many naive individuals in this nation, Branko?"

Be that as it may, the fact that he resented Communists did not by any means imply that he liked the occupiers, though, of course, the Communists had no intention of realizing the difference between anti-Communism and pro-Fascism. Whoever wasn't for the Partisans was automatically for the Germans – end of story.

Stavra was an anti-Fascist, a supporter of the Royal Serbian Army. Nothing could have been more natural. Whose side could a conscientious patriot be on in occupied Serbia?

Immediately upon their arrival, the Germans requisitioned Stavra's factories, though I am not absolutely sure that he was entirely excluded from managing his property; I do know that from time to time, he was summoned into the administration. I remember dropping by his house one day and being introduced to Mr Böttner, the manager of the plant for textiles, sugar, coal and wood – a man of high standing in the German power hierarchy. He was assistant to the German General Representative for the economy, Franz Neuhausen. I cannot say for sure, but I believe that Stavra was receiving some kind of compensation, not a small one at all, for their use of the factory. Both financial and material. I concluded thus because the Arandjelović household lived rather comfortably for World War II conditions, and because I know with certainty – Sima Rajković is my source – that Stavra contributed a great deal financially to Draža Mihailović and his Chetnik army. Before the war, you see, through his friend Stevan Moljević, Stavra had become friendly with the Serbian Cultural Club. Moljević also hooked him up with Mihailović. Stavra even attended the Saint Sava Congress in the village of Ba. "I have to attend," he said to me. "What else can I do? But I won't join their Central National Committee. I am a merchant by profession, a peasant at heart, my friend. I can't suddenly become a politician in my old age."

I understand Stavra's actions. He simply had to provide aid for the Chetniks. Although, I must say, I was not fond of Chetniks myself. I didn't even like them in the beginning, when their cause was rather sensible: they recruited the best people to fight the Germans, but their struggle was reasonable, they had consideration for the people. Theirs was not a resistance struggle that paid with a hundred innocent lives for every German railroad track destroyed in a Partisan sabotage operation. However, I got truly sick of them later, for no particular political or patriotic reason. As you know, Chetniks were both anti-Fascists and patriots. Rather, I disliked Chetniks for the same reason I disliked

Partisans: both groups recruited peasant scum into their ranks, our sorry, unbathed, savage Serbian peasants who hate the city, cityfolk, all matters pertaining to education, to industriousness and to everything even remotely above the hygienically and spiritually neglected larger remainder of the population. Gushing from two directions like a torrent, the vermin infested Serbia.

Here I glance at Bonehead – he's fidgeting around but doesn't say a word. His ears, in the meantime, are bigger than Dumbo's. The old man doesn't pay attention. His pretty sentences are noise-proof.

OLD FIACRE:
Stavra's perception of the Chetniks, however, was different. For him, the Chetniks were Stevan Moljević and the Serbian Cultural Club, Draža Mihailović, the war minister of the exiled Serbian Royal Government in London – the hero-giants waiting for the right moment to liberate the country from German and Communist scum.

Now what do you think, Miss Jelena, Mr Bilogorac – was Stavra Arandjelović guilty, or not?

BONEHEAD:
He's straight. You, Mr Doctor, you're wrong. The Serbian people ain't like that. It's got its faults but it ain't the way you describe it. Not the folk who fought the battles.

Uh-oh. I smell blood. Bonehead, of course, is mortified about the Serbian vermin thing. Insulted in the name of, according to the latest census – ten million eight hundred and twenty thousand three hundred and sixty-five Serbs. We're messing about with his friends the Terazije thumb-twiddlers with Indiana Jones hats and coquettishly crumpled collars. The insult is overpowering – Private Bilogorac is vexed but doesn't reach for his dinner knife, ladies and gentlemen! Indeed – he remains true to his image of part-warrior, part-Geodesist by remaining seated and merely sweating like a diesel machine. Kojović seems disturbed too – like, you know, he didn't mean it as it came out – Bonehead didn't understand him correctly, my apologies, bla bla. Of course, Kojović meant exactly what he said and Bonehead understood everything perfectly. Who are we kidding? Here I find myself in the role of diplomatic mediator:

ME:

All right, drop it. That's not the point. We're talking about the Arandjelovićs here, so let's stick with it. Here's another question for you, Mr Kojović: were Jelena and Jovan for the Chetniks?

OLD FIACRE:

No, Jelena and Jovan were snobs, which, in my humble opinion, isn't the absolute worst stance one can assume in this world. To Jelena and Jovan, the Chetniks simply reeked of the rabble, the common masses. They didn't want anything to do with them. Politics disgusted Jelena. She literally told me once: "Politics is the entertainment of the crude. It doesn't interest me."

Jovan, you see . . . Jovan was a slightly more complex case. Jovan would be what in my hometown of Klenak people sometimes call a "tin furnace". Intelligent, handsome as a prince and good-for-naught. He was a writer who had never published anything, though he did write a collection of poems. He read a lot and he knew all kinds of things – tens of stanzas from the oldest Japanese chronicle – the *Kojiki*, and in Japanese, no less! "How did you learn that?" I asked him, astonished. He replied that he had learned it through the German and English transcriptions of Japanese symbols. I didn't ask why – it would have been impolite. Jovan was simply a talented young man to whom the concept of utility was utterly foreign. Had I asked him why he had spent hours, days and months studying Japanese phonetics and orthography via German and English transcriptions, he wouldn't know what I was asking him. That was his nature. Unfortunately, the likes of him are judged all too hastily around here. Flotsam, they call them.

For years, Jovan had been toying with the study of great robberies of works of art through history. He could spend hours talking about Crusader rampages in Constantinople, the thefts of works of art during the Thirty Years War and the French Revolution. And thus, just as he had studied the Japanese chronicle "Kojiki", a mere few days before the onset of war, to his great misfortune, he tackled the teachings of Mita Ljotić.*

I still see him clearly: lonely, lackadaisical, defiant. On the day Cvetkovic† signed the Tripartite Pact in Vienna, I came for a visit and found him arguing in the garden of their villa, with the Marić brothers from the neighbourhood. Vladan and Radovan Marić, the sons of the phenomenally wealthy Jordan Marić, owner of large shops all over Yugoslavia, were Communists, and Jovan had got it into his obstinate head on precisely that day, to defend certain political ideas which greatly resembled those of Dimitrije Ljotić.

"More than half the territory of France is now in the hands of the Germans, dear friends," Jovan would say, badly concealing the resentment he felt for his interlocutors. "Poland has been partitioned once again, while Denmark, Norway, Holland, Belgium and Luxemburg are also under German occupation. Italy has occupied English Somalia, the Spanish have entered Tangier, Japan is bloating with military might, and Fascism, my dear friends, is spreading irresistibly whether we like it or not. The Communists are hypocritical and frivolous. The Communists are also anti-Fascists, but it does not seem to bother them that thanks to a pact with Hitler, Stalin has annexed Besarabia and Northern Bukovina, as well as Lithuania, Latvia, Estonia and southern Finland. These are facts. Nobody asked Prince Pavle if he likes this new world order or not. The divisions are being made as we speak, and while nothing is over yet, each sensible state must find in this new world the best place it can."

"Even at such a price, should we bear to live in a Fascist Yugoslavia?" the embittered brothers asked. Openly showing his pleasure at finding himself aristocratically lonely in his stance, a stance which acquires intellectual dignity precisely because it is championed by a few select individuals untarnished by the support of the plebeian majority, Jovan exclaimed: "And why NOT Fascism?"

---

* Serbian politician: passionate enemy of the Communists.
† Yugoslav Prime Minister 1939–41; stepped down when a military coup ensued after the signing of the Tripartite Pact with Hitler and Mussolini. The pact was intended to bring Yugoslavia closer to the Axis Powers.

I cannot cite Jovan's justification for the word – it's been too long – but I remember hearing him say that Fascism sprouted from the Versailles humiliation of a great nation which it was impossible to tie in chains. He also spoke of the strength of the Fascist movement lying in the readiness of the people to sacrifice themselves, their agnate dignity, their discipline of spirit, their ascetic pride and awareness of mission . . . the death of God gave rise to the Übermensch, while the West, ensnared in decadent selfishness and Platonic metaphysics, weakened itself, allowed itself to become a victim, and so on and so forth, to the same effect.

As expected, following this discussion, the Marić brothers labelled Jovan "avowed Fascist and Ljotić champion", though Jovan was neither one nor the other.

Politically, Jovan wasn't anything. Jelena knew that very well. Listening to Jovan with mild astonishment though very amused by his unexpected fervor, we both knew that he favoured Fascism at that moment because he was irritated by the Communist Marić brothers. As he later explained, he was that convincing only because he had recently been reading Montherlant's essays about Fascist Germany and Ljotić's *Message to the Fascist Apprentice* and *The Drama of Contemporary Mankind*, knowing thus how to stir some Fascism into Beumler's interpretations of Nietzsche and Schopenhauer and pepper it with his durable and passionate hatred of the Communist ideology of Collectivism and Anti-Individualism, creating a medley he was willing to savour only while it was hot.

"What's the matter with you?" Jelena asked when the Marić brothers furiously strode out of the garden. Still in the throes of oratorial zeal, Jovan replied: "I knew that those Communist fools would be infuriated if I sounded like a Fascist. I was right, wasn't I?" A while later, I asked him in earnest seriousness: "Jovan, do you believe, even remotely, in the superiority of the Fascists?" Psychologists have coined a term which best describes the behaviour of the then eighteen-year-old Jovan: "Juvenile insolence". Anyhow, he replied: " Of course not!" adding one magical, crucial word from his and Jelena's vocabulary: "What a bunch of vulgarians!"

Of course, Jovan never joined the anti-Communist "Zbor" nor any other organizations in occupied Belgrade. However, in addition to his argument with the Marić brothers (which would boomerang on him soon thereafter, when the brothers returned into Belgrade, victorious), his work with the Serbian Literary Collective and his meetings with Dr Hermann Werner Langhoff – a lieutenant in the political department of the German gubernatorial administration of Serbia – would get him into deep trouble . . . What am I saying – "trouble" is a euphemism, an entirely unsuitable word. I should say instead that the Marić brothers, the Collective and Langhoff were about to tear Jovan's life asunder.

In 1944, the Serbian Literary Collective bought Jovan's collection of poems *Thorns* with the intention of publishing it. It was considered unusual for the Collective to publish the work of a young man who hadn't ever been published before. People, depending on their inclination, began commenting upon this in two ways. The well-inclined interpreted the Collective's decision as a reflection of the quality of Jovan's poetry, while the ill-inclined tended to believe that the not-entirely-honest commissar of the SLC, Svetislav Stefanović, a friend of the Arandjelović family, counted on Stavra's financial assistance to boost the meagre budget of his publishing house. The truth, as always, lies somewhere in the middle. Jovan's poetry is very interesting, though one cannot hide the fact that Stavra offered financial assistance to Stefanović's collective. You can draw your own conclusions.

ME:

Do you have that collection, Mr Kojović?

OLD FIACRE:

No, unfortunately. Perhaps the manuscript can still be found in the archives of the Collective. But let me tell you – the Collective, even the ominous discussion with the Marić brothers, were mere missteps in comparison with, I shan't call it "friendship", but let's say, the "friendly encounters" between Jovan and the young Dr Langhoff.

You see, Jovan was a peculiar sort. Eccentric. Impulsive. Impudent. And crazy, according to some. Everyone agreed he was haughty, but I knew (and perhaps, apart from Jelena, was the only one to know) that he was merely trying to emulate Jelena's patrician hauteur and her aristocratic resentment of mediocrity. He never could. His effort at arrogance, unlike Jelena's, resembled a kind of nervous impudence, petulance, senseless irreverence. While Jelena was a born ruler whom conceit suited well, Jovan's irritable crassness towards others was the product of his insecurity and his fear of people. Though he was eccentric and brash, Jovan was an intelligent man – truly intelligent. Very oddly educated, I must admit, with the most peculiar erudition you're ever likely to run into, connoisseur of many obscure things, and full of resentment for systematic knowledge and learning. He boasted, for instance, not to know the number of continents nor the year of the Kosovo Battle. I believe it was partially an affectation, but there is no question that his education was full of gaps, left unpatched out of contempt for school and structured education.

That, more or less, describes Jovan. One loved him only if one truly knew him. I did love him; I was truly fond of the young man. Perhaps, Mr Bilogorac and you, Miss Jelena, are not yet quite capable of understanding that fatherly sentiment, or should I say – motherly, yet I always felt sorry for him. I couldn't exactly say why. Because he was so young, perhaps, so obstinate, wild yet vulnerable, endlessly vulnerable behind his high-and-mighty façade.

All the same, despite my sincere fondness for the young man and my familiarity with all the details concerning his rapport with Langhoff, despite the fact that I can testify to his unswerving patriotism as demonstrated in his conversations with the young German (I participated in several), the task of defending the foolhardy Arandjelović junior against the accusation of collaborating with the enemy would be a difficult one, even before a court infinitely more just than Belgrade's Communist court of law.

I do not know when and how Jovan made Langhoff's acquaintance but I know what connected them. Both were passionately interested in the great robberies of works of art through the centuries. They conversed in French and competed in a most pubescent way with their knowledge of the subject, which was colossal, by all standards. I listened, speechless, as the young German spoke in flawless French, in the middle of wartime Belgrade, and with an unbelievable familiarity

97

with the details, about the Roman leader Cornelius Lucius Sula, who, having conquered Athens in 86 BC, transported Aristotle's entire library to his house. He assigned two savants to study it: Andonicus from Rhodes, an interpreter of Aristotle's work, and the famous (sic!) Tiro. "You have certainly heard of Tiro, have you not?" Langhoff would nonchalantly ask, and Jovan, who didn't know the date of the Kosovo battle, would reply with matching nonchalance: "But of course – Cicero's personal secretary; he was the inventor of steno-graphy and used it to record all speeches made in the Senate." Intrigued by the mention of Aristotle's library but concealing that he was impressed with Langhoff's knowledge, Jovan would retaliate in equally exquisite French that Sula's requisition was not the first robbery of works of art in antiquity. With seeming indifference, he would remind the German of the great robbery in Volsinii of (if I remember correctly) 264 BC, when the legionaries transported some 2,000 statues to Rome, of the practical cleanup of Syracuse in 212 BC, and finally, according to Jovan's research, of the oldest art robbery of all, the robbery of jewels and urns in Praeneste in 380 BC. Listening patiently and periodically noting things down with his gold pen in a velvet-bound note pad, the young German warned his interlocutor about yet another, even older Roman robbery – that of the Etruscan mausoleum in Veii.

Hearing about Charlemagne and Theodorik's statue, the Crusaders' plunders in Constantinople, the famous (sic!) "Burgundy booty" – (never heard of it. Never heard of any of this shit, in fact), the disap-pearance of the painting collection of the English king, Charles I, the burglary of the summer palace in Beijing after the Opium War of 1840, and God knows what else, I was struck with the illusory impression that I was not where I was and that the reality which surrounded us – a ruinous Belgrade, the German occupation, a war raging all over the planet – had been mysteriously deleted. Not only was it an impression of unreality, I can now admit it, my dear young friends, but also a feeling of serious moral transgression!

ME:

Why?

OLD FIACRE:

Well, because an expert on works of art such as Dr Hermann Werner Langhoff decidedly hadn't come to Belgrade to compete with Jovan Arandjelović in his knowledge about great art robberies. Rather, he was in Belgrade to collect and take home to Germany from Serbia as much art as possible. When he was talking about the collection of King Charles, I barely resisted asking him about Prince Pavle's collection. Naturally, I remained silent. As you know, I am a convinced coward, but I am very sensitive to baseness, particularly in the behaviour of people I care about. There are moments in which aristocratic snobbery is well suited and other moments, when it simply becomes obscene. On that day in 1943, it was rather obscene of Jovan to be so basely unaware of the vile reality surrounding him and to discuss the statue of Theodorik from Charlemagne's imperial palace with a German! Everything in me protested the loathsome self-indulgence of the two young, passionate and at that moment, unconscientious men.

Don't think that I did not confront Jovan about this. I certainly did. Jelena did as well. Granted, she did so less forcefully, probably because she realized that knowing Jovan's adolescent stubbornness, our warnings would only be adding fuel to the fire.

I wasn't happy at all when following the liberation, Jovan started paying dearly, very dearly for his heedless adventures. The unpublished book of poetry, pro-Fascist arguments with the Communist brothers and the non-political conversations with the Fascist Langhoff were enough to provoke a few hundred students of the engineering department to beat him on the steps of the building where his trial was being held. He was imprisoned (fortunately, only for a week), denied food stamps and stamps for other rationed items, and logically, permanently prohibited from enrolling at the university. He was lucky enough to be sentenced to a mere three months of forced hard labour owing to the fact that the testimony of their maid Manda Jevdjic about the visits of Dr Langhoff, rather lacked credibility. The poor woman had a strong speech impediment and was slightly retarded. She never succeeded in remembering, among other things, the name Langhoff, and pronounced it differently each time. Secondly, she could not determine whether Langhoff was visiting Jovan, Stavra or Jelena, so that the deciding factor in the trial was the testimony of the supremely loyal cook Ivanka who lied that no such person as Dr Langhoff (Lagoff, Langhuff, Fuglann, Langfoon – as he was called by Manda. She also admitted at the suggestion of the investigator that his name was Turner) had ever set foot in the Arandjelović home.

There you are, children. That's the story. Those were the times. There are no innocent people in corrupt times. And there are no fair judges among the victorious nor among the defeated.

The old guy's getting tired, I can tell.

Children, can you understand those times and the humans in them? Can one understand an era one has not lived in?

ME:

Yes.

OLD FIACRE:

Is it different from yours?

ME:

Well, obviously, it's another era, but I wouldn't say it's different. Pretty soon the two could be entirely alike.

I uttered these conclusive sentences in my function as philosopher, social anthropologist and political futurologist. Christ. Am I full of it!

We leave the old guy. We've troubled him enough. And that rosé was a mighty fine narcotic. So we're climbing the stairs to my third-floor apartment ("lift *permanently* out of order"), and what happens: at the entrance, Bonehead's cane gets caught in the doorstep and he nearly falls over. Had I not caught him, he would've.

"A bloody cripple, that's what I am. I'm draggin' myself like a bloody sloth! I tell you, I'm fit for the scrapyard," he grumbles.

"I wouldn't trade you for two guys with both legs in working order." I'm sort of joking, though cross my heart, that's how I really feel. I love Bonehead seventy-seven times more than I love the fatherland.

"I'm a bloody wastrel, that's what I am," he continues in the same vein of muttering as I help him take off his pants. He's not usually like this – he's no moaner.

"Stop whining. What if they'd blown your leg to pieces, eh? They're taking your bandages off next week. Get over it."

"And then – rehabilitation. Two months, at least."

"Two months – two months. So what?"

"Well, you're right. That's my lot."

"I just hate the fact that we're broke."

"That's our lot too, I reckon . . . "

"If some dough miraculously landed at our feet, I'd take you to the seaside."

"Oh, I wouldn't go."

"And why wouldn't you?"

" 'Cause it'd be blasphemy! It would be a sin. People there are fighting and dying and we go to the beach? No, it ain't right."

"You wouldn't go to swim and play volleyball, my little hero, but to nurse your wounds. You sacrificed a litre of blood and a chunk of soft tissue for your fucking Moslavina."

"Don't tease, Jela, you know I'm not from Moslavina."

"Well, I just can't pronounce the name of that other place."

"Grubishno Polje. Why is that so hard to say?"

"I'm kidding! I know, I know. Grubishno Polje. At the foot of Bilogora, right?"

"Right."

"And Moslavina isn't far either, right?"

"Well, sort of. There's forty kilometres to Čazma, fifty to Kutina."

"And you decided to liberate all those territories, eh?"

"We've got no choice. That's where we belong."

"And what's wrong with here?"

"Nothing's wrong with here. Being around you is where I wanna be, but what are you gonna think of me sitting around your place, picking my nose?"

"Well, do something, if you have to."

"And what should I do?"

"Finish your Astronomical Geodesy thesis."

"I will, but first I'm gonna get my dead mum and dad's house back from those devil incarnates."

I take off all his clothes. His skin is white, healthy, tight as a drum. No fat in sight. And you know what? Bonehead's body kind of reminds me of Jesus', in Caravaggio's "Entombment". A nifty little painting. You see these women carrying Jesus down into the tomb and you can tell they know they have incredibly beautiful male flesh in their arms. Even the men, who are watching, know it. Jesus, meanwhile, doesn't have a clue. Or rather, he couldn't care less. He's the Holy Spirit after all. Flesh is the last thing on his mind. And really, if you look closely, that's exactly what Caravaggio painted: everyone's getting butterflies, except the nutty son of God who is tempting them. Well, Bonehead is like that too. He's got this godly body, and he doesn't even know it's there. He's not interested. He doesn't care that when disrobed, he's got the body of Caravaggio's Jesus.

"Tell me, Bonehead," I ask, "how many Croats, approximately, would you have to take out to get to your dad's house in Bilogora? I'm not asking for an exact figure to the thousand, you know, a thousand less, a thousand more, doesn't matter."

"We'll do to them what they did to us. But not now, Jela, OK? I really don't like fighting with you about this."

"And what do you like doing with me, my little piglet?"

"You know what."

We didn't argue. We did some of the I know what.

VII

Birdy's old man, a history prof at the university, arranged for Bonehead and me to look up what we need in the Archives of Serbia. The Archives, of course, are way the fuck off in the merry suburbs. My ultimate definition of hell on earth: sealed windows (lest we should catch pneumonia in the middle of the fucking summer), about 150 pairs of armpits. But after three days of communing with the unwashed masses, an hour there, an hour back, we compiled, from what seemed like three separate reserves, the entire court file of that loser of national honour – Stavra Arandjelović.

We, the author-researchers, now have the privilege of presenting our selected documents from the above mentioned file.

BELGRADE DISTRICT COURT
S. #259/44

Subject: decision on property confiscation re. Stavra Arandjelović

DECISION

By the verdict of this court #S. 259/44 of 12.04.1944, the state declares the confiscation of the entire property of Stavra Arandjelović of Belgrade. For the execution of this confiscation, letters have been written to the 1st and 3rd Municipal Courts of Belgrade as well as to the District Court of the city of Nish, for the confiscated property is located on their jurisdictive territories. A letter has also been written to the Serbian Ministry of the People's Effects into whose hands the confiscated property will pass.

Seal

Judge
(signature illegible)

COURT FOR THE TRIALS OF CRIMES AND VIOLATIONS
AGAINST THE SERBIAN NATIONAL HONOUR
S. #628/44

RECORD
of witness testimony
taken on 12.08.1944

PRESENT:

Court Clerk: Radmila Mokranjac

Investigator – district prosecutor: Bogoljub Popović

Witness: Tanasije Falkenberg
Occupation: Precision Mechanics Engineer
Address: 17 Dušanova Street
Nationality: Serb
Religion: Orthodox
Whereabouts during occupation: Belgrade
Sentenced – Yes or No: No
Related to the defendant – Yes or No: No

TESTIMONY

1. I have seen German officers drinking expensive alcoholic beverages with Stavra Arandjelović in his office a total of about twenty times. I know that one of the officers was from the Feldcommand; none of the others looked familiar.

2. I am aware that the worst merchandise of the factory was sold to our folk, while the best was reserved for German officers, with a discount to boot. We were told that Stavra Arandjelović gave that order when he handed the factory over to the Germans.

3. I think it was towards the end of 1943 that Stavra asked me to come mend the electric record player in his villa in Krunska Street because his son and daughter – Jovan and Jelena – had invited some friends over for a celebration. Since I am a precision mechanics engineer, I quickly found and fixed the defect. On my way out, around 7.30 p.m., I noticed that a German automobile drove to the entrance

of the villa and a German officer stepped out of the automobile. I asked who that was and somebody told me, I'm not sure anymore – maybe it was their maid, Manda – that it was Dr Langoff, or something like that.

4. By order of Stavra Arandjelović, I mended Dr Turner's electric heater and his electric stove. I also fixed some other Germans' various appliances.

5. I heard somewhere that Stavra gave half of his profit from the factory to Draža Mihailović, and that he once donated 500,000 dinars to the victims of an air raid in Berlin.

6. I heard from someone, I can't remember who, that in 1942, Stavra Arandjelović's son Jovan was seen near the town of Gornji Milanovac in a Chetnik uniform.

7. For the 1938 elections Stavra Arandjelović campaigned for Milan Stojadinović.

8. Everybody knows that Stavra gave an expensive Rosenthal dining set to a German officer for his birthday.

9. In January of 1944, I was welding a pipe while gas was going through it, when suddenly, the pipe exploded and the flame caught my eyes. I went to see prof Neshic and he told me that the operation would cost 15,000 dinars. I didn't have that kind of money so I asked Stavra Arandjelović for help. At first, he wouldn't give me anything, later he gave me two thousand. He gave pennies to a blind man and had hundreds of thousands for the Chetniks.

Everything I said is true and I am prepared to take an oath.

Witness interrogated by: Jovan Curcija (s.r.)

Witness: Steva C. Čolić, accountant, of 11, Admirala Geprata Street.

TESTIMONY

1. I believe it was towards the end of 1943 that I entered the main office and saw Stavra Arandjelović drinking cognac with Moteš – the head of the Textile Division of the General Deputy for the Economy.
2. I am aware that merchandise found in warehouses after the

occupation of Belgrade was sold in 1941 by pre-war prices to the following individuals: Moteš, the manager of the TDGRE in Serbia, Dr Fest, the German Controller in the Commissariat for Prices, and Major Hlavacheck. I don't know who gave the orders, but it was rumoured that it was our boss – Stavra Arandjelović.

3. On many occasions during 1941 and 1943, under the orders of Stavra Arandjelović and in agreement with the warehouse manager Patakovic, merchandise was secretly taken out of the warehouse and given over to the Chetniks of Draža Mihailović. For this crime, the warehouse manager Patakovic was executed in Jajinci by the Germans.

4. A few days before the elections of 1938, Stavra Arandjelović called for a general assembly of all workers in the plant and ordered us all to vote for Milan Stojadinović.

5. I heard from the Arandjelovićs' maid – Manda, I don't know her last name – that a German officer by the name of Foglan or Fogland came to dinner one night and that on that occasion he was presented with a Rosenthal dining set and a crystal vase for his birthday.

Witness: Djurdja Jovanović, cleaning woman, of 24 Dalmatinska Street.

TESTIMONY

1. Once, I think it was the end of 1943, when I came into the office to bring the coffee, I saw there a lot of German officer and Mister Stavra. Them all had glasses and they was drinking some fine drinks.

Witness: Jakša Drenovac, secretary in the firm, of 5 Jovanova Street.

TESTIMONY

1. I was familiar with the fact that Stavra Arandjelović held meetings in his office with the German officers Moteš and Turner and that they drank fine alcoholic drinks on those occasions.

2. Everybody knew that wool textiles and other merchandise were being taken out of the plant and sent to Draža Mihailović and that

it was the order of Stavra Arandjelović. The fact that Arandjelović was arrested and questioned by the Gestapo further testifies to that.

3. I am aware that Stavra Arandjelović was a personal friend of the traitor Milan Stojadinović.

4. I had heard that Dr Turner, the director of the Political Affairs Department of the Governance of Serbia, had had dinner at the home of the Arandjelovićs and that on that occasion he was given a Rosenthal dining set and a vase.

5. I don't remember whether it was 1941 or 1942, when Dragan Bogunovic, then a secretary in the firm and currently a sergeant major in our army, approached me and complained to me that the management of the plant had called the special police because the workers refused to load in a shipment of wood that had just arrived.

Witness: Sreten Vlajić, worker in the plant, of 12 Uskočka Street, Rakovica.

1. Comrade Milan Kalafatović, the accountant of the firm, told me that towards the end of 1941, Stavra Arandjelović paid a fine of 500,000 dinars for the disappearance of merchandise from the warehouse. The fine didn't come through the books as paid, because Stavra paid it as relief money for the victims of an air-raid in Berlin.

2. I once saw a tall German officer shake hands in a friendly way with Stavra Arandjelović in front of the plant. I was later told that he was a very important German official by the name of Turner.

3. Radmila Krešić, a former secretary in the firm, told me that sometime before the liberation, she saw with her own eyes Stavra Arandjelović's son dressed in a Chetnik officer's uniform.

4. I was told by comrade Milenko Djordjević, member of the National Liberation Detachment of the 2nd Region, that Stavra Arandjelović supported an entire detachment of Draža Mihailović's army with his own money. Its name was "Arandjelović's detachment".

Witness: Marija Radić, secretary in the firm; of 10 Majke Jevrosime Street.

TESTIMONY:

1. I am informed about the following since I paid frequent visits to the Arandjelović home: Stavra Arandjelović spent several months in 1944 in the interior. From a judge and friend of mine, I heard he had been to Racha Kragujevacka. I am convinced that his absence from Belgrade had to do with the activities of the army of Draža Mihailović.

2. I am also familiar with the fact that he presented a Rosenthal dining set and a large crystal vase to the infamous Turner for his birthday or name-day.

3. I also heard from their maid Manda Jevdžić, that the same Turner had had dinner at the Arandjelović villa.

4. Lastly, I heard from someone, I cannot remember whom exactly, that Stavra donated 500,000 dinars for the relief of Berlin's air-raid victims.

Witness: Jovan Stretenović, attorney in the firm, of 12, Jevremova Street

TESTIMONY:

1. According to the testimony of Milan Zimonjić, the Secretary of the National Commission for the Investigation of War Crimes in the 2nd Region, I am familiar with the fact that in February or March of 1944, a Chetnik conference was held in the village of Ba near Čačak, which the majority of Belgrade's wealthy industrialists and reactionaries attended. Among them was Aleksandar Krstić, the former head of the department for economy and parks for the City of Belgrade, for whom I once worked as a secretary. I know that the aforementioned attended the conference because I was told so by his brother-in-law Moses Milošević, the former head of department of Agriculture for the City of Belgrade. Aleksandar Krstić informed Moses Milošević of what occurred at the conference and that Stavra Arandjelović attended, along with other members of Belgrade's wealthy elite. As soon as I found out, I informed comrade Dusan Milošević of this. I am still in contact with him.

2. Organized comrades in Belgrade knew that the purpose of the arrests was to create the false impression that Draža Mihailović was

the enemy of the Germans and that Germans arrest all those who assist the Chetniks – hence Stavra Arandjelović. Their prompt release from German captivity further compounds that fact.

3. According to the testimony of the servants, a frequent guest at the home of Stavra Arandjelović was a young lieutenant in the Political Affairs Department of the Governance of Serbia, whom I have identified as Dr Hermann Werner Langhoff, an art historian who organized the deportment of works of art from Serbia. There is reason to believe that he was assisted in his endeavour by Jovan, Stavra Arandjelović's son.

4. Stavra Arandjelović was the personal friend of the Pro-Fascist prime minister Milan Stojadinović until the latter was expelled from the country.

There's enough testimonies here to clog a toilet – another forty in addition to the ones already printed here. The others say exactly the same stuff over and over.

Sod all, however, of defence witnesses to be found. Bonehead and I keeled over trying to find the witnesses Stavra wanted to testify. *Nicht. Nada.* "In the best interest of a thorough investigation", they were simply not called to testify, know what I mean? Those were: Toma Maksimović, the High Commissioner for Refugees, Djordje Petrović of 27 Vukovarska Street, Djura Radaković of 27 Hartvigova Street, Mileva Jeremić, of 26 Palmotićeva Street, Bogdan Blagojević, of 11 Vozdovačka Street, Petar Tomić, of 22 Krunska Street, and of course the servants, with the exception of Manda, a popular reference among those who did testify.

We will now present the last two items – Stavra's statement and his indictment:

Defendant: Stavra Arandjelović
Occupation: Industrialist
Address: 24 Krunska Street
Date of birth: 02.06.1885
Father's name: Miloš

Mother's name and maiden name: Savka, born Djordjević
Marital status: Widower
Nationality: Serb
Religion: Orthodox
Property: none (confiscated according to the verdict of the District
Court of Belgrade S.# 259/44)
Previously convicted Yes or No: no
Whereabouts during the occupation: Belgrade, worked as industrialist
Imprisoned Yes or No: currently in confinement.

STATEMENT

For a period of time immediately following the German occupation, I
managed from the head branch in Belgrade the firm Arandjelović
A.D. – both its Belgrade and Niš franchises. Towards the end of 1941,
the firm was requisitioned (and remained so until the end of the war)
and placed under the military management of the Textiles
Administration, only formally remaining under my management and
ownership. I had been ordered to give over all my buildings and
machinery, while remaining in the firm as adviser. All of the factory's
raw material had also gone into the hands of the German authorities
and I had been barred from all decision-making processes. In fact, I
had the status of a mere clerk.

During the occupation, I rarely ventured into the administration of
the firm. In fact, I went only when I was ordered to go. They did so
from time to time in order to maintain legal appearances. When I
came, I would run into the German officers Dr Turner, Dr Moteš,
Printz and a few others, whether I liked it or not. There might have
been a few others but I do not remember their names.

I must assert that these officers have never come to our house in
Krunska Street, and I do not know how our Rosenthal dining set ever
became the property of Dr Langhoff.

Untruthful are the accounts of those witnesses who claim that I
gave orders to Tanasije Folkman to mend Turner's appliances or any
other German officer's appliances, for that matter.

It is blatantly untrue that I was giving the best merchandise from the
firm to German officers because I was never in the position to do so.

It is also a barefaced lie that I gave any monetary contributions to air-raid victims in Berlin.

With the money I received as compensation for the use of my plant (a small compensation indeed, considering the true value of the capacities in use), I did contribute to the movement of Draža Mihailović, believing, mistakenly perhaps, that I was thus aiding the struggle against the occupying forces.

For these activities, I was arrested by the Gestapo in 1943.

I did go to the village of Ba, but not as a member of the Ravna Gora Movement. I attended as a patriot, not as a politician.

On the subject of my political stance during the occupation, I ask that the following witnesses be called to the stand: Toma Maksimović, the High Commissioner for Refugees of 17 Vukovarska Street, Djura Radaković of 27 Hartvigova Street, Mileva Jeremić of 26 Palmotićeva Street, Bogdan Blagojević of 11 Vozdovačka Street, Petar Tomić of 22 Krunska Street, and the servants who lived in the house during the entire period in question.

For the moment, this is all I have to say on this subject.

Signed

Stavra Arandjelović

CERTIFIED BY

Court Clerk: Assistant to the
district prosecutor:
(signature illegible)
Milivoje Mitić

The People's Prosecutor with the Court for the Trials of Crimes and Offences against the Serbian National Honour:

#259/45

May 18th 1944

THE COURT FOR THE TRIALS OF CRIMES AND OFFENCES AGAINST THE SERBIAN NATIONAL HONOUR

In accordance with article # 16 of the court for the trials of crimes and offences against the Serbian national honour, I present the following

Indictment:

Of Stavra Arandjelović, industrialist from Belgrade, of 24 Krunska Street, born on 02.06.1885 to father Miloš and mother Savka born Djordjević, widower, father of two children, Serb, of Orthodox faith, without property, previously unindicted, for the following reasons:

I His textile factories in Belgrade and Nish produced for the needs of enemy forces during the occupation of our country.

II He used the profits gained from working for the enemy to aid the Chetnik movement of Draža Mihailović.

III Having made the acquaintance of many Germans during the occupation of our country, he established friendly relations with the infamous Turner, the director of the Political Affairs Department of the Governance of Serbia, to whom Arandjelović presented a crystal vase and a Rosenthal dining set as gifts. He received his other German friends in the administrative offices of his firm, treating them to fine alcoholic drinks, selling them the highest quality textile products at a discount.

With this in mind, I recommend the following:

That the defendant Stavra Arandjelović be brought to trial before the Ist Council of the Court for the Trials of Crimes and Offences against the Serbian National Honour and that the following witnesses be called to testify:

(There's a lengthy list of witnesses here. Again, no defence witnesses are mentioned.)

PROSECUTOR'S CLOSING ARGUMENT:

By his own account, Stavra Arandjelović began his career modestly – as a quiltmaker's apprentice. With time, his name aquired repute not only in business circles but especially among the city folk of this country.

With regard to that, it was justifiably expected that at a difficult and portentous time, he would be on the side of the people. It was not so, unfortunately.

When our homeland was occupied and the enemy forces were killing mercilessly, plundering and destroying all that stood before them, when the national and moral responsibility of every citizen was to do everything in his power to liberate his country and his people, and that was possible only by means of National Liberation Struggle, the defendant, who before the war gained everything he had from his people, didn't do anything to liberate them.

In place of joining his people, he joined the enemy forces, gave a Rosenthal dining set to the infamous Turner, allowed his factory to produce for the needs of the Axis powers, and used the money thus earned to support the criminal activities of the Chetnik Draža Mihailović, who, in return, named one of his detachments of slaughterers "Arandjelović's detachment".

Stavra Arandjelović has thus proven himself to be the friend of the enemy of his people, which is to say – the enemy of his own people. He must be declared guilty and punished accordingly.

The defendant's claim that he was not involved in the work of the firm during the occupation is false, because he obviously spent time there.

The defendant's claim that he did not have friendly relations with officers from the enemy forces is unfounded – gifts are made to friends, not enemies.

Stavra Arandjelović must be punished for his misdeeds by the people, the very people he has harmed.

DEATH TO FASCISM – FREEDOM TO THE PEOPLE!

VIII

Am I going nuts? I don't get it. Bonehead can't be a total moron! This is how it is: I came home yesterday with truckloads of scoff. Scumbag sent five hundred in cash via some journalist from the New Zealand News Agency. Plus – the National Theatre paid me for the photos. Feeding time!

So I come in, I'm dumping the goods on to the kitchen table and what do I hear? Voices. A conversation. Bonehead's got company!

My first impulse, of course, was to go to the room and see what the hell is going on. But not so fast. In the spirit of investigative writing, I fetched my tape recorder, blessed be its inventor, and here's what I recorded for posterity:

CONVERSATION BETWEEN BONEHEAD AND THE
MOSLAVINIAN RABID DOG

BONEHEAD:

You can't die just like that! I mean, they gotta shoot you or somethin'.

RABID DOG:

Oh yes you can! 'Course you can. He killed her with his bare hands, he did. Buried her too.

BONEHEAD:

Jesus and Mary! How d'you mean?

RABID DOG:

He threw her down from the hayloft. Ripped her bloody kidneys out, fa chrissake! She took a whole month to shove off.

BONEHEAD:

That animal. He's a fucking rabid dog, that's what he is. And such a damn good woman she was! I tell you, he should've been taken in a long time ago. So what happened, did they catch him?

RABID DOG:

Whad'you think?! They catch him every other day, but getting outa' lockup these days is as easy as falling off a log!

BONEHEAD:

And?

RABID DOG:

Nothin'. He told 'em she fell off the ladder by herself and died.

BONEHEAD:

So whatya gonna do now? Are you gonna marry Milica? Are they even gonna give her to you now that your uncle's killed her mum?

RABID DOG:

Are they gonna give her to me?! When a Serb wants somethin', he gets it, buddy. That's the way things are now. Anyway, real fighting men don't marry so long as there's a war.

BONEHEAD:

You know what? Damn this war and damn all those who started it!

RABID DOG:

Just listen to yourself! You sound like some grandmother. A little scratch on the leg and mister educated smart arse is shitting his pants! Ha! Let me tell you – what's going on now is a picnic. There's no rules. What you couldn't dream of doing before, you can do now. Sounds like fun to me! My own old man is scared of me!

BONEHEAD:

Makes sense. You've fucking slaughtered hundreds by now.

RABID DOG:

Maybe, but I left your folk alone. Never touched a hair on their heads.

BONEHEAD:

You know something? It's because of guys like you that we're made to look like beasts. Stay away from me, d'you hear me? You butchered people with those hands!

RABID DOG:

I didn't butcher. And if I did, so what? If they're not Orthodox, they don't deserve to be spared. I'm telling you, I'd rather blow a Croat to bits than win the lottery!

BONEHEAD:

You know that there are good people among Croats.

RABID DOG:

Uh-oh. Looks like the Belgrade scum've sucked up all your brains!

BONEHEAD:

Oh yeah? Looks like blood has made you blind as a mole! You can't see a human being from all the killing you've done. You know full well there are good folk among them.

RABID DOG:

Not a dog's chance! And if there is?! Whadya want? You want them to wipe us out? Is that what you want? What kind of a man are you? You don't get pissed off at anyone! You're not a man, you're a chicken!

On hearing "You're not a man, you're a chicken" I decided to make my entrance. I couldn't let this one go by. Calling my Bonehead a chicken! I was pretty sure that Rabid Dog was built like a water buffalo, six by six feet at least, but then again, Bonehead is quite a wild beast himself, and the least I can do is kick him in the balls and bite off his ear. When, lo and behold! Not even water buffalos are what they used to be! Rabid Dog's a twig! A wretch – as Bonehead put it. His chicken chest is hiding inside the coarse wool sweater he's wearing on naked skin. He's balding, young, all crumpled up and miserable, his two front teeth are missing, two tiny little cheeks swimming in a pair of humungous camouflage trousers. So when I saw him, I entered a state of total confusion: how can I beat him up if he's barely alive?

Bonehead got pretty frantic too. He started waving his arms around like some schizoid traffic cop:

"Jela, this is Joko Martić, neighbour from my village. This is Jela Panićeva, my girlfriend."

When I heard Bonehead calling me Jela, my anger vanished into thin air. Suddenly, everything seemed hilarious. Jela Panićeva! What a joke! If I'm the property of my daddy, Mr Panić, why wouldn't Rabid

Dog be the property of Mr Martić, the gentleman who's afraid of his professional butcher son? Talk about fucked up family. Since I had eliminated the option of beating twiggy up, I asked:

"So you are Martić's Joko? Old Martić's baby?"

Rabid Dog looks at me. Insidiously, suspiciously. Just like an actual rabid dog when you offer it a bite, and it doesn't know if it should approach you or stay away.

"So, you say, old Mr Martić is scared of you?"

He didn't answer. He didn't get up from his chair. He wasn't quite getting the idea, but he could tell it wasn't good. He didn't look like he knew what to do, so he gave Bonehead one of those frantic looks. A disgusting species all to himself, this guy. Never seen anything like it. Shall I give him a good beating anyway? While I was weighing my options, I asked Bonehead:

"Does this guy have any language skills?"

Bonehead gave no answer, so I persisted:

"Or does he merely bark when a stranger approaches?"

Bonehead answered angrily:

"Look Jela, stop messing around, OK?"

So I walked over to Rabid Dog. I practically got in his face and said:

"Listen to me, my little pussycat," I divided all my words into neat little syllables and pronounced everything slowly. "I'm going to ask you one mooore time: are you the baby of the goood old mis-ter Mar-tich, or – are – you – not?"

Rabid Dog glared at me with the same look of suspicion on his face. He wasn't about to snap.

I suppose I misjudged him. Really misjudged him. And I realized only when it was too late. Only when the emaciated sleaze lazily got up and walked around me (he couldn't very well go through me), casually pushing me out of his way with his hand. He pumped up his belly, tightened his arms like a muscle man and for some reason, skinny as he was, he didn't look funny when he said:

"Some shit even when they don't have to. Some fucking life!"

He said that as you might say "When you see a piece of shit, it's

117

best to go around it" or "these days, everyone's acting like they're all-important", or something like that. Then he grabbed his hat and blew out, leaving the front door open.

A megaflop, admittedly. Did I beat him up? No. Did I teach him a lesson? No. The fucking butchering bastard.

Silence. Neither of us says a word. We roam around, supposedly doing chores. Bonehead picks up the ashtray and the glasses from the table, empties the ashtray, washes the glasses. I stock the fridge, take off my shoes, look for the slippers . . .

"I can't stand to see his face. I can't even stand the thought of him," Bonehead says after a long pause.

"How d'he find you?"

"Somebody told him. Somebody in Hotel Serbia."

"So what's he looking for here?"

"Trouble, as usual."

I pace around the place a bit more. I don't know what I'm looking for, but I know it's something. Finally, I go up to Bonehead. I grab him by the ears. I make him turn around and look at me:

"Look at me. Listen carefully to what I'm going to ask you. Don't turn away! Don't fucking turn away!"

He's up to his elbows in soapy water. He says:

"Don't swear. You know I don't like it."

I have to stick in a little non-sequitur here. Something about my Bonehead. Something I've known for a while.

Bonehead doesn't like it when I swear, because, as he claims, when I swear, words are not swearwords – they mean what they literally stand for. Bonehead will swear here and there, but it's different when he does it. His swearing plays the function of an exclamation, it doesn't mean a thing. It's got no colour, no flavour, no smell – it's like the noble gas, Helium or something. But he'll never utter an obscene word himself. And he hates it when I use one.

For example, sometimes, I'd say "I gotta scratch my cunt" 'cause I do! Shit, is that the end of the world? He turns all red, jumps out of his chair, makes some kind of sick expression, like I'm sticking mustard up his nose! Where did this chick grow up, in the jungle!? Didn't her mother teach her anything better? Yeah, yeah.

Anyway, once, we were talking about customs, superstitions, stuff like that. In his area, at the foot of the Bilogora, he says, when you see a Catholic priest and you want to protect yourself from the omen, what you have to do is:

"You gotta grab your . . . " he says and stops there.

I realize of course that the mighty dick is in question, but I prod anyway:

"What is it that you have to grab?"

"The . . . ahm . . . the lower aspect of your sexual organ," he says, impressed by his unexpected resourcefulness. I can just see it: the wizardly act of grabbing the "lower aspect of your sexual organ"! Whoa! I imagine a Bilogora fart prancing around the valley and meeting a Catholic priest. Instead of saying "Praise Jesus", like all decent human beings do, the Serbofart grabs the "lower aspect of his sexual organ" to fight the omen! I crack up laughing, of course, what else could I do?

"Is it the head you grab?" I ask again, when I've caught my breath, but sweetie pie implores:

"Fa chrissake, Jela! Don't say those things. It ain't right for . . . oh Jesus and Mary! Just shut your gob, OK?"

So that's what we need to know here.

But this is about something else. He knows it too.

"Don't swear. You know I don't like that," he says, just to change the topic. But I'm not letting him. We're not kidding around this time. We're not talking heads and dicks here. I know. Somebody hit me if it isn't true that this time, it's about all of him, all of Bonehead.

Jesus. My temples are scorching. I'm pulling on his ears with all the strength I can muster. I'm looking right into his eyes, but he's fidgeting around:

"Rabid Dog came to drag you to the front, didn't he?"

"No, he didn't."

"You're lying!"

There I catch him looking, so I say it again:

"You're lying!"

"I'm lying," he says, dejectedly.

What the hell do you do in a situation like this? Can't kill the bloke. Can't tie him up. I keep thinking: He won't do it. I know he won't. Bonehead isn't that deranged. No one, except Rabid Dog, is that deranged.

We didn't mention Rabid Dog again.

We thought about him.

Incessantly.

I asked (so I have something to ask) what we should stick into chapter eight. We've been wondering about that for the past week. Bonehead scratches his head and examines the Inventarium Helenae.

"We could . . . we could finish off Jovan."

"I think so too. Where did we leave off again?"

"Right here. I marked it."

"We should type it up."

"I'll do it."

Bonehead types.

I read the handwriting on the wall.

JOVAN (3)

I was certain the end was drawing near when, with no warning and without a subsequent word of explanation, Jelena brought Krsman over for tea.

Target day.

Zero hour.

In this operation, Jelena is the supreme commander. But, with Krsman's permission. He voluntarily relinquishes himself to her charge. He has his reasons, his shrewd peasantly calculations. He accepts being under Jelena's protection because . . .

But more of that subject in a while. The gift of observation and conclusion-drawing would return to me later, much later, for in the first few moments of their arrival, I did not see anything clearly. Sights were blurry, as if submerged in water. Words travelled my way silenced; I strained my hearing to distinguish them. I behaved, I talked, I listened to Jelena and Krsman, but my comprehension of the words we exchanged was delayed. I first answered questions and only later realized what I had uttered, yet not even at that stage was I able to connect words with images. Sights seemed to spill over the space taken by uttered words. Words flew over the sight of blurry outlines.

I cannot better describe my mental state, and it's no wonder that this description is vague, rigid, lacking in focus. Amidst the wide variety of my somnambulic adventures, the mental state I was in when confronted by Krsman under Jelena's protection occupies a very special place. It cannot be constructively compared to my acute narcoleptic condition nor to any of my later experiences of drifting in the dark. Thus, I speak of the first ten minutes of our encounter only on the basis of subsequent vaguely and chaotically recollected details.

One of those details was Krsman's reply to Jelena's question. I cannot remember the question. Nor can I remember Jelena's way of posing it. But knowing the reply, I conclude that she had offered him tea. The white teeth and bronzed cheeks stretch into a grimace. The slightly hoarse, insolently cheerful voice speaks:

"What do I need tea for?! I'm not sick!"

For a moment, Jelena shines very clearly in my memory. Her voice is clear and resonant. She says:

"You will drink tea."

Then plummeting. Flat out. In a spiral. And the continual echo of Rimbaud's stanza as translated by Jelena:

> Those are seas (you are the sea)
> Following (me), the solar flame.

There is no more. Only that stanza, though I know the entire poem by heart. And that stanza about Jelena (the sea) and me (the flame), about the sea extinguishing the flame of the sun and the sun singeing the watery sea, not even that stanza touches anything around it; it too plummets spirally with me, with a whoosh into nothingness, dividing into two entities and becoming one again. One new, incomprehensible entity. At times it reads: "Those are seas, following the solar flame." At other times: "You are the sea, following me, the solar flame." And then again: "Those are seas (you are the sea) ... " The stanza and I are feeling something hard, a bottom, perhaps. The chair. It's his chair I am sitting on. A cup of tea is in my hand. The haze in my head is dissipating in irregular bursts like mist dispersed by a mild wind which capriciously changes its course.

I finally see them clearly.

I see Krsman:

Grimacing white teeth, shiny black eyes, like two stove burners polished with sandpaper. They blind me, yet behind their shallow glitter I sense (but do not comprehend) a dangerous abyss. He is slouched down in the chair stretching out his strong, long legs. From time to time, I can see him leaning the heel of his left foot against the toe of the right, revelling in the gloss of his polished boots.

I wondered what I should do. I heard myself saying:

"What will happen to Stavra Arandjelović, colonel?"

It sounds unbelievable. I, who for weeks, even months, was desperate and disgusted at Jelena's consultations with the barbarian about plans to free Stavra, was now, in essence, following in her footsteps. There was no logic to my behaviour. Nor was there a motive. I did not call Krsman "colonel" to flatter his ego – artful dodging was above my head at that moment. Nor did I pose the question because I really wanted to know what would happen to Stavra. I don't even think that I was fully cognizant of my question. The force speaking through me was beyond my control. In fact, only subsequently would it appear strange that I, precisely I, asked the colonel about Stavra's destiny and that the comrade lieutenant colonel, which he really was, tolerated my accidental faux pas with no visible signs of discomfort. In that instant, however, I discovered an unexpected power in my question, because it extinguished the grimacing smile on Krsman's face with the quickness and ease of a magic wand. My discovery filled me with a sudden, healing self-confidence. A cloud of distress gathered above Krsman's dark face. He rose from his chair and stated sombrely:

"I'm doing all I can."

And despite my enormous resistance to the conversation, something in me continued:

"Could you be a little more precise?"

Krsman glanced at Jelena. As she gave him no encouragement nor a sign for the direction in which to proceed, he managed on his own:

"I get his letters through. He received his heart medication."

"Do they no longer beat him?" I asked further, now completely healed and in the mood to lay traps:

"No."

"So they did beat him before you intervened?" I continued defiantly.

"I don't think so. They don't beat people in our prisons."

"Really? And what do they do?"

"They separate the chaff from the grain."

"And we certainly hope that Stavra is, shall we say – grain?"

Krsman paused. His next reply suddenly sounded different – secret police-like, ambiguous and threatening:

"We certainly do, Comrade Jovan, we certainly do."

My heart was absent from this conversation. I faked deep concern and hidden anger over Stavra's fate, but I was utterly conscious of my cheap and superficial arrogance. I felt ashamed for several different reasons at once, but only later would I be able to dissect the sludge of frozen malaise undulating in my entrails: I was ashamed to be talking to Krsman at all; ashamed because I knew all along that I was much less concerned for Stavra's fate than I would like it to appear from the insincere rage of my sentences; ashamed to be taking advantage of my father's predicament in order to conceal the true reasons for my disquietude – the fear, the awesome fear that I was losing Jelena.

I see Jelena:

She sits glacially still. Unnaturally composed. Nothing more. From her expression, none save I could guess that she was following the conversation or registering anything at all. Her hands, folded in her lap, reach in equal intervals for the cup of tea on the table. Single-mindedly committed to her peace, she performs that action with the same single-mindedness: she thoughtfully brings the Rosenthal cup to her lips, takes a sip and puts it back on the saucer.

But, I know.

Jelena seems to don her steeliness and her glacial exterior only when she is seized by panic on the inside, panic strong enough to escape her if not kept down inside the regimented body. Jelena's appearances cannot fool me, however. I can tell: the material Jelena is made of is on the verge of tearing. Jelena is ashamed and frightened. Ashamed of Krsman. Frightened of me. Afraid of what I could do, at any instant. She is afraid it might be something irrevocable, though at that moment, neither she nor I have any idea what it might be.

Nonetheless, the power to extinguish the gaping grin on Krsman's face and the awareness that I was in better shape than panic-stricken, glacier-like Jelena, re-established some sort of flustered equilibrium inside me. The fog dispersed.

I see myself:

I am sitting in the middle of the sofa, towards the longer end of the rectangular coffee table, my legs drawn together like a virgin's. I am full of yet unnamed nausea. I am holding the saucer in my left hand and the cup in my right. I am not drinking my tea.

To discontinue the discussion about Stavra, or for some other reason – breaking the silence perhaps, the awkward silence gathering above us after virtually every sentence, Krsman began to recount a rather roundabout story from his youth – an adventure from his shepherding days, about some kind of licking salt accidentally diluted by rainwater. He merrily ridiculed this recollected trouble, as he was now regally superior, vastly distant, both temporally and socially. I cannot remember the entire story – I watched him more than I listened to him. His body spoke to me in a more comprehensible language than his words, which penetrated my consciousness only as the background music of Krsman's world. Those sentences which stick in my mind, I remember as music, not as elements of his tale. I remember their sounds better than their meaning.

He did not doubt his charm for so much as an instant – satisfied with his body at every moment, pleased with every word, incredibly conscious of his biceps, his sunken stomach, his aggressively flaunted pelvis, his lovingly outstretched legs; shamelessly vulgar and convinced that his gaudy theatrics were irresistibly delightful. A loud, handsome "hero", thrilled by himself and by his life, a life which suddenly metamorphosed into an unending feast of the victorious.

I see Jelena again:

Hands clasped. Eyes lowered.

On my back, I felt the sweat trickling down her back. Her glacial back. I felt the cold wetness of her sweat. And I rejoiced (may God forgive me if He exists and if He can) at the thought that Jelena and I were suffering. Good, I thought to myself. She deserves it! We deserve it! May God punish us even more ruthlessly. May God populate the entire world with the grotesque offspring of this insensate hour – I thought, and heard in those words traces, false traces of course, of a kind of justice I did not understand, making a tentative appearance in my befuddled mind as the soothing possibility of a way out.

I too need consolation. Even if it is a pack of lies. I'm only human.

I began to sense that even Jelena, Greenlandian Jelena, was nearing the breaking point. With the intention of fairly dividing up the remainder of her forces, she disclosed her cards prematurely and blurted out the reason behind Krsman's visit.

"Krsman wishes to ask you something, Jovan."

She looked at Krsman:

"Isn't that right, Krsman?"

"Yeah, yeah, I do. I just thought you was going to ask him before, Jelena."

"I haven't asked," she said, barely suppressing the rancour in her voice. "*You* ask," she commanded.

Jelena was the commander, beyond any doubt. But she was so with Krsman's approval. I did not have the time to formulate my observations into words, though I knew that behind Krsman's façade of submissiveness lay an arsenal of provincial shrewdness and authentic peasant treachery: "Sure, go ahead, just go on ritzing it, my little peacock," he seemed to be thinking, "I'm a hard nut, I can take it, but I'll knock you off your perch soon enough."

On the surface, however, he couldn't have looked more obedient.

He promptly executed Jelena's command.

"Nothing much to say, actually. It's like this: if I wanna, I can get your Senjak house, the one the Germans took from you."

I remained very calm. The news was unexpected, though it didn't affect me at all. They had confiscated our world. What was one house less or more? Yet, almost instantly, I felt physical discomfort at the thought that our rooms, which always smelled of us, would be desecrated not by some nameless barbarian, but by one whose physical presence in our bathroom, dining room, bedroom I could imagine in all its concreteness.

"Get it . . . from whom?" I asked.

Krsman showed his practical side:

"Like this: I was assigned a house in Rumunska Street. This one in Senjak – your house before the war – well, that one was first assigned to someone from the City Council, to Mutapović or Jankez, I don't know for sure, it don't matter really. What's important is that it's now under the control of the deputy government of the DFY. I asked them guys in the provisional government if I can exchange my house for the one in Senjak. They said yes. So I can."

"What is DFY?" I asked.

"Democratic Federative Yugoslavia," Jelena mumbled through her teeth.

"And why are you telling me all this?" I asked Krsman with genuine bewilderment.

"Well . . . Jelena would like me to take yours . . . "

"Jelena would LIKE?" My question jolted like an echo. Jelena stared at her lap, mutely.

"Right, Jelena?" Krsman continued, "I mean, there should be no misunderstanding. I just wanted to ask you too."

"Do not ask me anything," I replied after a lengthy pause.

Dead silence. A long dead silence. Then I articulated a sentence which was a surprise even to me:

"I hate the People."

Krsman looked at me blankly. He didn't understand a thing. I turned to Jelena:

"Jelena, shall I tell Krsman about your last encounter with Radoje from Ripanj?"

She didn't say a word. Her gaze remained fixed upon her clasped hands.

As no response was to be extracted from her, I addressed Krsman:

"Radoje is a peasant who used to bring us cheese, poultry, eggs, in exchange for suits, porcelain, jewellery and such. He was so high and mighty, so full of himself, mister-lieutenant-colonel . . . he seemed to be avenging himself on the city, skinning the backs of the gentility with great pleasure: Stop moping, missus – he would say, his grin stretching from ear to ear, his ego swimming in a sentiment of total superiority. All right, alright, give us the stuff. Our five minutes have come, I tell ya! Your days are over, Arandjelovićs! Us peasants are now the kingpins in this country. All right, All right, give over grunting. Here's another egg. And do you know, Comrade Krsman, what this missus finally replied? Tell him Lena. Don't be such a hardhead, tell the gentleman what you told Radoje from Ripanj."

"Bad move, Jovan, against the rules," she said, her gaze still fixed upon her clasped hands.

"Against the rules, Lena? You are the one to talk about rules? Now? This is not the game of Literary Deceits, Lena, you know that full well! There are no rules in this game. The rules have been cancelled, dear! The world continues to turn in different directions, at different speeds.

"Here is what Missus Jelena told Radoje from Ripanj, Mr Krsman. She said: 'Go back to your pigsty, you filthy hog.' And I, mister-lieutenant-colonel, knew exactly what she'd said even before the door slammed in front of the nose of that Radoje fellow. I had discerned everything. Clairvoyantly. Every single one of Jelena's words. As if I had spoken them myself. I understood it all just as I understand – nothing! Not a single word! It's as if her silence is a set of hieroglyphic symbols, not yet uncoded by Champolion! Bizarre, truly bizarre. Tell me, Mr Krsman, tell me honestly, don't you find it strange? And you, Jelena? What do you think of all this? Don't you think it's strange that I am unable to decode a single one of your unuttered words? I, who . . . "

This was the end of the road for Jelena. She could tolerate no more. She prevented her own complete breakdown by rising from her chair, abruptly – like a jack-in-the-box, and nervously declaring:

"We have finished the tea . . . " – a rather disagreeable message to our guest that the visitation was over.

As Krsman briskly rose to his feet, I thought for the first time that the conversation may have seemed awkward even to him, that even he realized the artificial circumstances under which we pretended to openmindedly discuss the possibility of Krsman taking our house in exchange for another, that house also confiscated from someone. The world had been sprained, the world had evidently popped out of its own joints. At that instant, however, I was not thinking about the world. Krsman occupied all my attention: I couldn't see the wood for the trees.

The promptness with which Krsman obeyed Jelena's command to leave revealed that behind his façade of nonchalant vulgarity, there were small traces of awkwardness, after all. Or am I fooling myself? I don't know. If he did feel awkward, even in the slightest degree, perhaps he isn't "the most ordinary" barbarian. I recalled yet another of my conversations with Jelena dating from the beginning of January:

"He isn't quite ordinary," Jelena said.

"Who?" I asked.

"The Communist barbarian. He is beginning to manifest certain human features."

"Krsman?"

"Yes."

"Human?"

"Well, let's say human*like*. Parahuman."

After seeing off the parahuman baker, Jelena returned to the room. Not immediately. I know that she stood at the door, composing herself, gathering her strength. Finally she came in, quietly, plucklessly. Like a pickpocket, she walked by me, straining not to meet my eyes. She huddled in the armchair by the tile furnace, turning her back on me. She drew her knees close to her chest and hugged them with her arms (that is precisely the way she carried her books on her way to the Gymnasium, a blue beret with the number of her class, 5-2, sewed in gold letters covering her hair. This girl in the blue uniform, this lean, lonely girl lost in a sea of chattery girls, was my lover). Her chin sank into her gripping knees – something I did not see, but guessed from the position of her head. I watched the nape of her neck and the arch of her bending spine in the dead silence of the room. As usual, I knew what she was thinking, to the minutest detail: she doesn't know what to say, she doesn't know how we are to continue our lives, she is frightened, she is sad, she would cry, she is angry at not being in complete accord with a single one of her emotions and at not being able to conceal a single one of her thoughts from me: she feels sorry for me, she feels sorry for herself, she hates me, she hates herself, but most of all, she hates Krsman.

Though I knew all that, her troubled contradictions somehow bypassed my full awareness. I did have Jelena's heartache in mind, but I didn't have the time to be concerned with it, for the panic enveloping me was more urgent, mightier, irresistible, unshakeable. It literally deafened me: I only heard the resonant wail of silence. It felt most like anger, this onset of panic in me, most easily transformable into a triumphant feeling of just revenge. The desire to be rough was growing like a new organ in my body, later shaping itself as words – scathing, numerous, impatient, uncensored. My gaze fixed upon the sight of Jelena rocking in the chair with her chin glued to her knees, rocking evenly back and forth like somebody's wooden horse. I was making a great effort to contain the outburst of words, to resist their onslaught. I gripped my teeth and clenched my fists but to no avail – they erupted like a natural disaster, charged and unbridled:

"What do you need the house for, Jelena? Every house they appropriate transforms into a barn, Jelena!" I screamed louder than I could bear. "They smell of decay, they kill their ailing fathers with shovels and we plead with them to free our Stavra?! They wipe their arses with their fingers and rub them off on walls, they feed their fires with pages from the Testament, they care for their cows better than for their

129

women because they are stronger and cheaper to feed. Wake up, Jelena! They sing like howling wolves, they don't read, they're infested with fleas and rabies, they will kill for one penny, they will take out their brother's eye in the name of Marxism, they will plough over the streets of Belgrade to be reminded of their native villages, Jelena! They fart in church, burp at the table, fuck sheep, draw cunts on icons of the Madonna! They are thugs, Jelena, you have to under . . . "

"Stop it! Stop it! Stop it! STOP IT!!!" she howled, covering her ears with the palms of her hands. She rolled to the floor, shaking. Tears streamed down her face. She repeated the same words over a few more times, each time more quietly, until finally, the syllables transformed into soft sobbing:

"Stop it, stop it, please, stop, stop . . . "

In reading this, one must consider the following: Jelena rarely cries and there is nothing in the world which I find more difficult to bear than Jelena's tears. I can count her adult crying bouts on the fingers of one hand; I also remember each situation in which she cried, the duration of her crying, the type of crying it was, the reason, the place. Regardless of whether her crying was my fault, hers or somebody else's, I experienced each one of her crying bouts as a personal failure, as ultimate proof of my worthlessness. Reason went out the window in those situations. While Lena cried, all connections with reason were temporarily suspended. All I knew was that I was ready to do anything at all, even the craziest of things, just to stop the tears. Immediately. Before I went insane.

And on that day – on the day when on Jelena's suggestion, Krsman announced that he would generously move into our house, Jelena's tears halted the river of obscenities gushing out of my system, though they did not bewilder me as much as they had, in situations past. I cannot quite say why, but this time, I tolerated her crying with greater composure than before. I approached her, knelt down on the floor, hugged her. I even started crying myself. But I knew where I was, who I was. I didn't feel the insatiable need to stop the crying immediately, nor did I feel personally humbled by her distress.

It was then that, relatively conscious of my actions, I covered Jelena's breasts with my hands.

Why had I done it?

The closeness of ailing souls? The closeness of our physical bodies? Desire?

Perhaps. Tragedy had precipitated us into one another's embrace. The fullness of her flesh had indeed aroused the nicest and most painful memories in me. I wanted to feel the white softness of Jelena under me once again. But I would be lying if I said that desire was the sole determining factor for my behaviour. Hundreds of times in years past I had experienced moments of total spiritual intimacy with Jelena, I had wanted to touch her breasts and hold her close to me countless times, yet I always restrained myself.

Why didn't I do so in this situation? Why did I not stop even when Jelena nervously, coarsely pushed my hands away, decisive and firm, and said:

"Don't act like a child, Jovan."

Had it only been a question of desire, the firmness of her rejection, the audible tone of indignity and the hidden hint of disgust in her voice would have certainly stopped me. I continued nonetheless, fully aware of what I was doing and why I was doing it:

Jelena kicked, gasped, sobbed, wailed, while I calculatingly worked towards forcing her to have intercourse. I tore off her pants and hiked her skirt up to her throat. When I penetrated her with the fingers of my left hand and unzipped my fly with the fingers of the right, she managed to reach for the teapot off the coffee table and swing it against my temple with all her might.

The blow was strong – blood instantly covered the side of my face. My mind was in a whirl, but that did not stop me from carrying out my intention. Realizing that I would not give up, Jelena gave in.

We did that act in silence. Precisely that – we did it. We did it as some might do their morning exercises.

I rolled off Jelena's immobile body. I touched the blood rolling down my neck, stupidly perplexed by my bleeding. Our heavy breathing was the only sound in the room. I secretly looked at Jelena. She rose.

She straightened the tatters of her shirt, lowered her skirt and collapsed into the chair. She looked at me. I cannot describe how. Emptily.

I sat on the floor, cleaning the blood off my temple and neck with my sleeve.

The breathing gradually grew quieter.

Without looking at her, I asked calmly, softly:

"Did you sleep with him?"

She didn't respond.

I knew she had.

From the very beginning, from the second day of Christmas nine years ago, I have been unable to think of our love without simultaneously thinking of death. I said that aloud:

"I cannot think of our love, Jelena, without simultaneously thinking of death."

After a brief pause, Jelena replied:

"Death isn't the worst thing in the world."

"What is worse?" I asked.

"Poverty. I will never be poor, Jovan."

I am lying in my room, uncovered, in the dark. I sense Jelena on the other side of the wall. I am wakeful in her sleeplessness, I think her thoughts, my heart beats in accord with hers. I am bestially awake. My head is perfectly clear. I know everything. What was. What will soon be. I see the future so clearly that at times, it seems more certain than the past. I am frightened by the clarity of the image, the sureness of my clairvoyance. That which will happen in two or three hours I see in greater detail than what happened two or three hours ago, the ugly and unforgettable act between me and ruffled, tattered Jelena on the floor.

Awake and united with sleepless Jelena on the other side of the wall, I know that she too, thinking about us, thinks about nothingness, that she too hears as I do, the machine-gun fire of her heels taking her from me into Krsman's inconceivable world.

The sound of machine-gun fire wanes. I look up at the sky above Belgrade, white as a bride's veil, and I know what to do.

THE END

Voilà. The "The End" here is my addition. That's all, folks. That's all that Uncle Jovan ("Uncle Jovo" in Bonehead's dialect) has left for us. Twenty-six single-spaced pages, which makes about fifty after we've retyped it. We have finished with his treatise. Jovan can no longer assist us in reconstructing the love life of Granny Jelena.

A sentence beginning with "poor Jovan" lingers at the tip of my tongue, but I have no time to utter it. Bonehead is quicker: "What a wretched human being," he says.

That said, I swallow my insecure little opinion. I am not sure what he was. Jelena and Jovan will not be worse or better off because of Bonehead's spoken or my unspoken thoughts. After all, Radoje from Ripanj was right when he said: "Your days are over, Arandjelovićs!"

IX

Last June in "The Blue Rider", Kojović told us about Slavko Vrcalov. This Slavko bloke apparently spent time in the nick with Stavra. Seven or eight years ago, his address was 11 Jovana Djordjevića Street, Kraljevci. No phone number. Kojović has no clue if Vrcalov is still there, if he's alive at all, though he should be – he is about ten years younger than Kojović.

So I tell Bonehead:

"It's worth a try."

Bonehead says to me:

"It is."

Well, in theory. Autumn came and went and we didn't even get organized enough to send him a card. Mind you, Bonehead had been nagging me all along, so finally, in October, he wrote a card in my name: "I am the great-granddaughter of Stavra Arandjelović, I'd very much like to know about the old man's days doing time, bladibla . . ."

Soon enough, Vrcalov wrote back: he would gladly see us, he's always home, we can show up whenever we feel like it.

Said – done. It's the beginning of November and Bonehead and me are on the Trans-Siberian railway line Belgrade–Šid. There's nothing beyond Šid, mind you. Šid is the end of the world. From Šid to Vrcalov's village, tanks play the role of public transportation.

The Trans-Siberian chug chugg-chugg stops at every lamp post. Batajnica, Indjija, Old Pazova, New Pazova, the Newest Pazova . . . a fucking tour of the dumps of south-eastern Europe!

We're alone in a freezing, piss-infested compartment. Bonehead covers me with his anorak.

"Don't, Bonehead. You'll catch cold."

134

"No, no. I'll be OK."

The sweetheart. I give him a kiss on the cheek. This causes an outburst of tenderness in him, and he asks:

"Do you love me even just a teeny bit, Jela? Would you marry me?"

The guy knows the answer, of course. He's asking rhetorically, just fishing for those soothing love words.

My turn to ask:

"Bonehead, seriously: Why do *you* love me?"

"Because you're a pretty and honest girl."

God. What a joke!

"Pretty? Let's be realistic here. I'm fat."

"Well, I just love you as you are," he continues, "it's quite easy, loving you, Jela. I've never loved anyone like that before. Not my dad, not my mum, not any other girl. I love you because you're different. I love you because you can't do a thing in your kitchen to save your life. There ain't no life for me without you. Or for you without me. We're alone in this world, you and me. We only got each other."

Where's my tape recorder? Bonehead's talking crap and for the first time, I don't feel like jumping out the window! In-fucking-credible! Maybe it's because I like what I'm hearing. And because of the way Bonehead's saying it. He's totally sincere. It's all straightforward, clean, like a geodesical equation or something. The guy is establishing simple facts, explaining the current state of affairs.

"We'll live a nice life. I'll always wait for you clean, shaved, the house'll be neat and everything'll be just swell."

"What about the war? Will you go to the front?"

Silence. Screeching halt. He gets up. Looks out the window.

"I mean, you tell me you love me, but the truth is – you're going to leave me."

"I'll never leave you."

"How about when you get shot, you little twit?"

"I ain't gonna get shot."

"They're dying like flies, Bonehead! They're dying by the thousands!"

"Well, of course. Of course they're dying. Everyone has to die some day. Man stepped into his grave the day he was born."

I'd mush him like a cockroach, honest to God, if I could live a single day without him, the wally!

Silence again. Each pondering our own shit.

We finally arrive in Kraljevci, the sprawling metropolis and cosmopolitan capital of Europe. Jovana Djordjevića Street is at some distant corner of the village, muddy as the tropical rainforest. We're walking along and sinking. Quicksand, man . . . Everywhere you turn, there's miserable little multicoloured houses that look like they've been transplanted off a kid's drawings . . . Deadly boredom. Quiet.

"Look. Ain't it pretty? So quiet . . ." Bonehead marvels at the sights.

"Oh, give me a break!" I snap, still fuming about the "Man stepped into his grave the day he was born". The necrophiliac.

Number 11 is a pallid blue house, and a thick wall painted the same colour surrounds the courtyard. There's a wide gate for cars and cattle made of rotting wood, its remaining scraps held together by wire. Beyond the gate is the entrance to a large porch which stretches along the entire side of the building. That door is falling apart too, grinding against the brick below – Bonehead had to prop it up with his shoulder to open it. To the left side of the porch, there's a door leading to the interior of the house. To the right is the door to the courtyard, a junkyard of history: a pile of debris, enormous plastic pots – paint peeling off them, a rusty ploughshare, a broken wheelbarrow, the back seat of some old carriage – springs sticking out through the punctured leather. The entire courtyard is panelled with bricks, still more or less holding together. A couple of ducks (ducks! The first and last time I saw ducks was in my nursery school colouring book!) are picking at the weeds growing in between the bricks. There's a semi-collapsed corntrough (we later learned from Vrcalov that that's a structure used for drying corn. It has a concrete foundation and walls made of separated laths so air can circulate through. Ah, to learn, to learn! One learns something new every day – I could've died unenlightened by that essential word – "corntrough"!). Two of the four windows facing the courtyard have glass, two are boarded up.

I hear a pig oinking.

On the box: "An afternoon in the country". A rerun from 2 p.m.

Vrcalov looks different. Not much similarity between this guy and the flowery, ornate handwriting of the letter we received. A fat, provincially dingy old man. You'd never think he was once "a law student, son of a wealthy peasant, a Belgrade gent", which is how Kojović described him. You can tell by looking at the kitchen that he lives alone. The cheerful fire in the wood stove stands out against the general murkiness of the whole dump. And the dump stinks. Muchly ("Muchly"! Where the hell did I pick this one up?) The stench is a mix of vomit-inducing smokiness and prehistoric mustiness. Seems like the place hasn't been aired since February 1946, when they released Vrcalov from the slammer. The oilcloth on the table has seventeen burns on it. ("D'you see how many holes there were in the oilcloth?" I asked Bonehead on the way back. "Seventeen," replied my little astro-geodesist. "How d'you know?" I asked. "Counted them.")

Vrcalov brings out some pork crackling on a shoddy enamel plate. He slices three pieces of bread and places one in front of each of us. We must be hungry – long trip and all. He goes down the steep staircase leading to the cellar and returns a moment later with a jug of wine. Souer wine. A concoction akin to that Slovenian poison they call "Cvicheck".

Just like five o'clock tea.

Vrcalov seems to be trying to remember gentlemanly manners from his Belgrade days, but without much success. Once a peasant, always a peasant.

A good afternoon to you from Bonehead and Bulika, your literary explorers at a wine and crackling tasting party in the Serbian interior.

A dog barks.

A pig oinks.

We begin our investigation.

I switch the tape recorder on. Bonehead and I will later select the best segments for the book. Edit we will, but we won't add anything new, as usual. With our assistance, the book writes itself.

VRCALOV (1)

ME:

Kojović told us that you know how Stavra Arandjelović ended his life.

VRCALOV:

Everybody knew that: he hanged himself with a skein.

ME:

What's a skein?

Vrcalov and Bonehead answer in a chorus:

BONEHEAD:

String, twine.

VRCALOV:

Rope. Now, I bet you'd like to hear me say that Stavra was a sweetheart of a man. Well, let me tell you – he wasn't. He wasn't bad, no, but then again, he wasn't as a man ought to be. What I mean is, if you rose from rags to riches you can't be squeaky-clean. That's what I reckon.

They say that he earned it all with his own hands. That's a load of horsefeathers, that is. Other people's hands, other people's sweat, they meant. He'd suck you dry, like all of them bosses. It was hard to earn his dinar, believe me.

ME:

You worked for Stavra before going to jail?

VRCALOV:

Oh no. I had nothing to do with industry and trade. Me, before the war, I was studying law. During the war, I was chasing girls around Belgrade, running from Communists, Germans, Chetniks, everybody . . .

ME:

And why did the Communists arrest you?

VRCALOV:

In '44?

ME:

Yes.

VRCALOV:

God only knows. They were arresting every mother's son in those days. Of course, they claimed I was collaborating with the Germans, which I wasn't. If I was, I'd say so today. No skin off my nose! Nobody gives a tinker's damn about that nowadays. In '43, I did spend some seven or eight months (I had no choice – my dad's allowance had dried up) working for DIRIS.* I just worked as a clerk, distributing coupons to people for food rations. "Collaborating with the enemy", my eye. Someone must've split on me – that at least was as easy as ABC in those days.

ME:

So how do you know that Stavra was a slave driver?

VRCALOV:

He must've been – to start off as an apprentice and end up with such riches, you had to. And then, you get to know a man when you eat the same bread and sleep in the same room with him. In jail you can't hide what kind of man you really are.

ME:

And what kind of man was Stavra?

VRCALOV:

Stubborn as a mule. Harsh. Harsh with himself and with others. I don't like that in people, I have to admit. Yes, he was a tough nut to no end. We'd tell him, me and the others: "You have to stop speaking up for the Chetniks, Master Stavra. That's like rubbing salt into these blokes' wounds!" He wouldn't hear about it. He just kept ranting: "Draza was an honest man, Draza was an honest man." "By God, forget Draza now, Master Stavra. Look out for your own head!" No use. He didn't seem to know where he was and who he was dealing with. Stubborn. Stiff as a di . . . oops, excuse me language, Miss Jelena.

This has got to be a widespread phenomenon in the countryside. Not even Vrcalov can say the word "dick".

I offer assistance:

* Food Distribution Administration.

ME:

. . . the lower aspect of the sexual organ?

Vrcalov's confused:

VRCALOV:

Huh? What d'you say?

BONEHEAD:

Oh, nothing. Nothing. (Bonehead retorts, paranoid that I'll come up with something worse.) She didn't say nothing. She's just . . . just teasing me about something.

ME:

So how exactly was Stavra toughnutted?

VRCALOV:

Well, I'll give you an example. Of course, we were all very hungry in jail. Not just hungry, starved, dear missus. Often, we were thirsty too. Those animals wouldn't even give us water to drink sometimes. "Die, vermin!" they'd say to us. In the beginning, we couldn't even receive packages, so in the morning, you'd get a piece of mouldy bread and a bit of hot water they called coffee. At noon they'd give you a soup with a couple of leaves of cabbage in it, and if you were lucky, you'd find a bean or two. There wasn't any fat to speak of in that muck!

Then, one morning, a miracle! Master Stavra got a package and a letter. He read the letter but he just wouldn't open the package! And you know what he said when we asked him why? He said he didn't want to be different, and why should he be the one to get a package when no one else can. Somehow, we convinced him to open it and even so, he distributed everything in the box except his heart medication. Now you tell me: wouldn't you call that being a tough nut?

ME:

I'm not really sure what that is, but from what I can see, he was useful to you guys. He gave you food.

VRCALOV:

Yes, yes, you're right, Miss Jelena, but I got to tell you something: I don't like people who pretend they're saints. When I meet a saint, I run as far as my legs will take me. With the kind of higher justice they're after, other folk around them take the blame, not them. Especially in jail. You see, when you're a free man, you can do whatever suits your fancy. Not in jail. In jail, nothing's your private business 'cause everyone's responsible. If he'd rejected the parcel, for example, everyone would've paid for it, the whole cell would've been punished. But Stavra didn't much care for that. That's why I said he was a tough nut.

In jail, you just can't act special. Master Stavra, for example, didn't want to, excuse me – defecate in front of others. I know, it isn't exactly pleasant. Even I, in the beginning, had to hold it for three days straight. The cell was teeny, four people in it, I couldn't do it in front of other people's noses. But you get used to it. After a while, you stop noticing that others are listening and looking. And the others are not listening or looking anymore.

ME:

And how did Stavra shit if he couldn't do it in front of the others?

VRCALOV:

Don't ask. A whole bloody strategy it was. The siege of Stalingrad must've been easier to plan. Firstly, I'd go to the common toilet – six holes one right next to the other; the space was so small people were bumping their arses, excuse my language. So, I come in and give a cigarette to everyone in the toilet and ask them to clear out. Then, while Stavra's evacuating, I'm standing by the door and giving a cigarette to anyone who wants to go in. If they want two, I give them two. Just so Stavra can do his business in peace. If nobody's disturbed him while he's on the bog, I get five cigarettes myself. That was like a pot of gold for me. 'Cause you know, in the nick a cigarette will get you anything.

ME:

And where did Stavra get all those cigarettes?

VRCALOV:

He had a good connection. An OZNA* colonel.

ME:

Krsman?

* Department of Defence for the People (actually secret or political police).

VRCALOV:

Yeah. Colonel Krsman Jakšić.

ME:

Did you know him?

VRCALOV:

I didn't know him. But I saw him. Twice. The first time, briefly. The guard opened the door, stood to attention, and that colonel, Krsman Jakšić, came in and started looking around the room. We all jumped to our feet, took off our hats, eyes down. We all did everything by the rules, except again, Stavra, who'd decided to piss against the wind. So instead of looking down, he stared at the colonel. Sima the commissar whispered into my ear: "He'll fuck up. I tell you he'll fuck up." Excuse the language, miss. But he didn't. That's what I mean. I would've fucked up, but not Mr Stavra.

You know what those Communist gits say? They say we're all equal. Well, that's a load of crap. Why then would an OZNA colonel address Stavra with "sir"? "Are you Stavra Arandjelović, sir?" he asked. And when Stavra confirmed it, he told him to follow him outside. We were all crazy happy when they left the room, 'cause an OZNA colonel, in those days . . . Can you imagine what that title meant? Well, no, of course you can't. If you can imagine what God means – well, the OZNA man was a little higher up than God. He could kill you, he could save your life, he could do anything!

ME:

What did Stavra tell you when he came back? Was Krsman going to save him or what?

VRCALOV:

To be honest with you, I don't know. There was plenty of behind-the-scenes gossip about that. Yes, it's true, he wanted to help Stavra. As to why he wanted to help him, there were two stories. According to one, during the war, Stavra made the OZNA man obligated to him by saving his life. Apparently, he bought him off from the Germans with pure gold. So the story went. According to the second version, and this one was more in circulation, the Krsman fellow was bonking Stavra's daughter. I don't much believe that one.

ME:

Why not?

VRCALOV:

Well, you see, the kind of man Krsman was just doesn't fall in love. And if he does, he throws fathers and husbands in jail, just to get the poor daughter or wife to lift her skirt. That kind of man is incapable of helping others. He's only capable of taking away. They were beasts, his sort, I tell you. But then again, I don't know about that Krsman fellow, as an individual. *Exceptis excipiendis.* Maybe he was different, the exception proves the rule. Apparently, that daughter of Stavra's was a real beauty. Milena, Milena was her name I think . . .

ME:

Jelena, Jelena was her name.

VRCALOV:

Jelena, you say? Possible . . . well of course, you know better than me what your grandmother was called. Right. Anyway, it was believed that the colonel was visiting Stavra because of her, getting his parcels through, calling him "sir". Can you believe it? An OZNA colonel calling a prisoner "sir"?!

ME:

And why didn't he help him through to the end? Why didn't he get him out?

VRCALOV:

That's something nobody knows. Not me or anyone I knew. But there's somethin' else. Something only I know about Stavra. I haven't told a soul, but I'm going to tell you two. I kept my lips sealed all these years, and when you hear what I was hiding, you'll understand why.

ME:

Stavra confided in you about something?

VRCALOV:

Hold your horses. I'll tell you everything in time. First, why the colonel didn't save Stavra's life: If an OZNA colonel didn't want them to sentence Stavra, why did he let it happen? I found that sort of odd. And not only that, but to let them sentence an old man to ten years of

143

high security imprisonment with forced labour! But then again, it's possible that the colonel's yellow-eyed Communist grudgingness kicked in – he couldn't help hating a Capitalist – you follow me? It's also possible that even he as colonel couldn't do much, that Stavra was too big a fish. If they'd confiscated all those factories and lands, how were they suddenly gonna prove that Stavra wasn't a war criminal? And if you're a war criminal, you get at least ten years, not a day less. With forced labour. It wasn't fortunate being rich in those days, children. My own father, nothing but a common peasant with barely fifteen acres, and they skinned him alive. And if they snatched from a nobody, they sure as hell will snatch from Stavra Arandjelović, the richest man in all of Serbia.

ME:

So, d'you reckon Stavra killed himself because of the sentence?

VRCALOV:

That, I can't know. I know he killed himself on the day his appeal for a shorter sentence was turned down. So, you work it out.

BONEHEAD:

Can I ask you something Mr Slavko? Stavra hung himself with a rope, right?

VRCALOV:

He did.

BONEHEAD:

You see, I know for a fact that the moment a man goes to jail, they take away his shoelaces, his belt, his tie, any thread he may have, anything he could use to hang himself. So my question is: how is it that Stavra had rope in the clink? Wasn't it against the law?

Bull's eye! Vrcalov sparked like the fucking aurora borealis.

VRCALOV:

Ha! Now we're talking! That's exactly what I knew and kept quiet about. Half a century, almost. Forty years I couldn't speak, and now that I can, it doesn't matter a hill of beans that Stavra had rope in jail! Since you are the first to ask, you'll be the first to know: the rope Stavra tied to the bars of the window of our cell, and then used when he jumped from the pisspot and died, that same rope was given to him by Colonel Krsman Jakšić!

In-fucking-credible! That's what I'm thinking to myself. Agatha Christie in the heart of the Balkans. The crucial witness whose testimony nobody gives a hoot about anymore. Except, of course, Bonehead and me.

BONEHEAD:

Why Krsman! Did he want Stavra to kill himself? Did Stavra ask him to bring the rope?

VRCALOV:

That, I don't know. You're the first to ask. Nobody cared back then. Back then, they only asked who gave him the rope. I was the only one to know, but I kept my mouth shut.

BONEHEAD:

And how d'you know?

VRCALOV:

Saw it with my own eyes.

ME:

What did you see?

VRCALOV:

Well, it happened so that Master Stavra and I were once again in the same cell, our beds next to each other in the Mitrovica jail as well. It's possible that it wasn't just chance – that Stavra asked his colonel friend to put us together. I was young and strong, and he was an old man, so I helped him out with everything. Stavra trusted me, and I admit, I had some use from him too. Anyway, on that day, our cell was on cleaning duty and Stavra and I were assigned to clean the walkway. So we went about our business, sweeping, picking up rubbish and dumping it in the bin, when suddenly, I hadn't even seen him coming, but there he was – Colonel Krsman Jakšić. He greeted Stavra formally; didn't even look at me. I thought to myself: I better clear out. So I kept sweeping, but far away from them so I couldn't hear what they were talking about. I could see them clearly, as clearly as I can see you two now. My eyes were young back then, so I couldn't have been wrong . . .

And boy, what did I see – Krsman looks around to see if anyone is watching, then he takes out of his officer's bag some thingumabob wrapped in newspaper and gives it to Master Stavra. Master Stavra quickly sticks it under his prison shirt, and that's the end of that. Never entered my mind at the time that it could've been rope. Cigarettes – I thought – bacon, maybe long underwear . . . something of that sort, you know.

ME:

You're sure it was rope?

VRCALOV:

Stavra hanged himself on that day. What else could it be, I ask you, and where else could Stavra have got rope?

BONEHEAD:

Mr Slavko is right. It couldn't be anything else . . .

ME:

But why did Krsman do that?

BONEHEAD:

We don't know, Jela. At least, we got something to think about.

Bonehead is right. We got something to think about. And that's what we did on the way back. We trudged in silence through the quicksand of Vrcalov's neighbourhood until we reached the asphalt of downtown Kraljevci. Civilization! The twenty-first century – fucking unbelievable!

God, I can't get over this thing. It sounds absurd, twisted, I don't know: Stavra got the rope from Krsman? It doesn't fit what we know, but somehow, I'm cool as ice about it. I'm not even making an effort to work it out – why? Why the hell did Krsman do it, who told him to, did he do it with or without Jelena's knowledge, etc. . . . .

So instead of thinking about that, as every normal literary researcher would, another question I don't understand is wreaking fucking havoc with my brain, and even if I did understand it, I wouldn't have the balls to utter it in front of Bonehead because it's simple and it goes:

"Why the fuck are we doing all this?!"

A stupid question, of course, because I know the answer. But somehow, the answer suddenly seems even more stupid than the question.

So I keep my mouth shut.

And I think about Bonehead's recovery. Another ten days of rehab left. Tops.

"Could be longer," he says.

"And then?" I ask.

No answer. But I know what then: there goes my dingdong, conquering the Bilogora mountain, while I'm left to psychoanalyse the long dead lovers of my long dead granny. God bless their demented souls and whatever. A fucking mess.

Again, we are lucky with an empty compartment in the Trans-Siberian chugg-chugg Šid–Belgrade. This time, however, it's scorching. Sauna. The Gobi desert.

So, we peel off the layers, we make ourselves comfortable. And still, that burning question of mine won't stop bugging me. So, finally I edit it a bit and I ask:

"Bonehead, tell me something. Why are we doing all this?"

"What?"

"This. Of all the places in the world, what the hell are we doing in this fleapit backwater of Kraljevci?"

"Well, it's our book, right? We gotta finish it and we don't know how things ended. We're researching. Filling gaps."

"But why?"

"What do you mean – why? We know why."

"Well, if you know, tell me, because I don't."

"Well, first of all, to write our book, and second of all . . ."

"Second of all?"

"So you know who your grandpa was."

"Krsman or Jovan, you mean?"

"Krsman or Jovan, yes."

We travel in silence. Newest Pazova, New Pazova, Old Pazova. In Batajnica, I proclaim:

"I don't give a shit."

"What about?"

"Whether my grandfather was Krsman or Jovan."

"Oh come on, Jela. Now, I can't understand you anymore, not even a bit. You can't not give a shit about whose blood flows in your veins."

"I don't give a damn about blood."

Bonehead reflects for a minute, then asks (curious yellow):

"And what would you like better, Jela – to be of Krsman's or of Jovan's blood?"

"I don't give a shit whose blood I have, I told you."

"Still, uh? Come on!"

"Of Jovan's, for the time being."

Bonehead reflects again, and says:

"And I'd like you to be of Krsman's."

"You little mountain freak. You are positively deranged. You're really rooting for the bad guy, aren't you?"

"I don't agree. Krsman ain't a bad guy."

"And what is he? Fucking Erasmus of Rotterdam, perchance? A Renaissance Humanist?"

"My dear Jela, all of them – Stavra, Krsman, Jelena, Jovan – all these people from our book are unlucky souls in an evil time."

That's what you get when my Bonehead gets reflective. Sweet as pie. I give him a kiss. He smiles, innocently, like some little calf (calf!) and asks:

"Jela, why do you love me?"

"'Cause you're a handsome and honest boy," I reply seriously. Worriedly, like some old spinster.

X

"My dear, dear Jovan" – those are the opening words of Grandma Jelena's letter found in the canvas bag aptly named Inventarium Helenae by my Latin-loving super linguist.

Is this promotion, or what!

Hence (as Kojović would say), here's the letter, although my logic-obsessed astro-geodesist was firmly against putting it here (the explanation will come later).

JELENA'S LETTER

My dear, dear Jovan;

The world no longer exists.

I have travelled through its remains, by train, from the sordid Belgrade railway station to the battered Gare de Lyon.

Enveloped in the locomotive's smoke and surrounded by OZNA men, the train taking the Yugoslav delegation to the peace conference in Paris waited for us on platform one. It reminded me of some sort of private carriage. There is no set time of departure, you see. We shall depart when everyone gets on and when the hobbling Slovenian, bolt upright on the front seat, yells to the coachman: "Onward!"

My commemorative journey through what used to be the countries of Mitteleuropa lasted for three days and three nights.

For as I said, dear Jovan, the world simply no longer exists.

In a town once known as Feldkirch, women, hunched over and unaccustomed to physical labour, are pushing carts loaded with debris from the ruinous train station to the neighbouring meadow, where more women are assembling large pieces of construction blocks into neat, dusty piles. One of the ladies layering the bricks is wearing white satin gloves; her naturally red hair is half grey.

On the outskirts of Innsbruck, I saw the tail and the wing of an American Flying Fortress sticking out of a four-storey ruin.

In the wheat fields of the valleys of Carvendelgeb, the Cielertaller Alps and the Tuxers, like a flock of fallen birds, old men, women and children are rummaging for seeds through the stubble left after the harvest.

In railway stations of the Europe which no longer exists, in place of kiosks selling breakfast rolls, frankfurters, flowers and wreaths, in place of delightful girls dressed in Tirol national costumes running after your train, offering lemonade and wild strawberries in cones made of leaves, the trains are now awaited by maimed people and children, asking for bread and cigarettes in different languages:

"Brot, bread, ham-ham, pane."

In front of the Landeck train station, in the scorching midday heat, a long row of hunched people are slowly moving towards a cauldron where a woman, her hair pulled back with a dirty white napkin, is filling the bowls of these poor souls with hot soup. When the cauldron is emptied, two old men take it down. They seem to barely have the strength to lift the full one up to the hook. As they do so, the hot liquid spills to the ground and on to their legs and sandals.

We look out on to a non-existent world through the filthy windows of our compartment. We eat chicken out of newspapers, jam out of glass jars covered with cellophane and tightened with sticky waxed rope. We drink water hurriedly drawn from hoses sticking out of the ground in deserted railway stations like the skinny necks of some peculiar species of bird with brass taps in place of beaks.

Brana and I are standing in Heiligenblut, on the grounds of the burnt-down, charred railway station. The railway station as well as we, who for two nights and two days have been dried by the smoke of the locomotive, are black as cinder. Dirty. Exhausted. Sweaty. The contact of my own two hands with one another disgusts me. We are stretching out our stiffened legs and our compressed spines.

Brana glances at our train and whispers to me, though we are all alone:

"The freight train for the transport of Communist diplomatic excrement of the New Yugoslavia."

"With us in tow, dear Brana," I add.

"Travelling on a collective passport. A passport in the pocket of Vladimir Dedijer," concludes Brana, dejected.

Had you been there, had we been alone, I would have allowed myself to cry briefly. Since you were not, and I was not alone, I returned to my scorching compartment and the moth-eaten, stained, tattered red plush of my seat, the seat which stands for everything smuggled from a world now defunct into the one being built now.

The tattered seat. A leftover relic from the Orient-Express, a migratory hotel de luxe I travelled in seven years ago, young, convinced that reality was absolute for all time and that it was the reality of my comfortable and warm sleeping compartment and of the restaurant with glisteningly white tablecloths and sterling silver cutlery. The tattered, red plush orphan with no one in the world, with no father or mother, with no master or keeper, travels through the devastated railway stations of Europe, while former ladies from Feldkirch in white satin gloves are piling bricks or, as the case may be, translating copies of peace treaties from French and English into Serbian, for the barbarians.

There is no more world, Jovan. Rest assured; that at least is certain. One great certainty amidst a sea of petty uncertainties.

Of course, there is no more Paris either.

We naively believed, for four solid years, that Belgrade, Paris, Europe, that the whole world was in hiding. We believed it was holding its breath and – waiting. Waiting for the moment when all the bells of all the churches of the world would announce that the war was over and that everything would return to normal that very instant. "The Majestic" would once again be scented with expensive French perfumes, coffee and rum, the Orient–Express would transport refined gentlemen and elegant ladies politely letting one another through in the narrow corridors of the carriages, making as much room as possible at that, the gothic cathedral in Köln and the National Library in Belgrade would rise from the ashes in all their pre-war entirety, intact.

In other words, the world would awake unchanged from its period of hibernation, and continue its forward stride from the spot where six years ago, it fell into a deep winter sleep.

Alas, it is not so, dear Jovan.

In the Hotel "Céramique", I am served a dark mushy bread called "pain national" and a cup of "café national" for breakfast. Marmelade is not "marmelade nationale" though it is made with sacharin. Margarine is served in place of butter. Soya milk in place of milk.

In my room, withered like the face of a long outdated beauty queen, the carpets and brocade curtains have moulted, the "Cheval" mirror is cracked through the middle, the gilt peeling off on its frame. Rusty brass of the bath and bidet taps. No trace of a bath. No shower. No hot water either. Patched up linen on the bed. In the metro, there is no first class, only "Classe Nationale".

The world, dear Jovan, the entire world has been nationalized. At the "La Motte Picquet" stop, where I transferred for Trocadéro, just as I did seven years ago, the nationalized crowds in cheap canvas dresses and crumpled trousers, sweaty under their armpits, are thoughtlessly crowding into the packed, stuffy carriages of the train.

The sterling teapots and red carpets, the crystal chandeliers and the opulence of the old world in the Palais du Luxembourg where the conference is being held, and the Café de la Paix, where one can enter only with a special pass for the high officials of the anti-Hitler coalition dividing up the wealth of defeated Germany, Italy, Rumania, Bulgaria, Hungary and Finland – they make the misery outside of these oases of luxury even more conspicuous.

Leaving our Partisan-ridden Belgrade, I believed, dear Jovan, I believed that I was travelling to a world which would contradict my dreariest suspicions: that there is no return, that our world has disappeared forever. Unfortunately, I must notify you that my suspicions were justified. Communist Belgrade is hell, beyond any doubt, but the rest of the world will not be returning to its previous condition either. I believe that in a few years' time, Paris' national marmelade will once again be made with sugar and that coffee will once again be imported from Brazil, but all that cow's milk, all that genuine butter will be consumed by a hopelessly nationalized, vulgarized, homogenized people whose needs and tastes massively coincide.

Hitler was not the one defeated in this war, Jovan. We were. You and me. We are the biggest losers of this war. Not because they confiscated Stavra's houses and factories but because they confiscated our world, a world in which it was possible to live as we pleased and differently than prescribed by the crowds intoxicated by their new rights in the new state of equality for everybody and everything. A young French author, Albert Camus, the most talked about writer and a popular philosopher here (something akin to Bergson during the twenties or Nietzsche during the war), calls egalitarianism "the Calvinism of democracy".

He is right. He who decides to go on living will have to do so in a world constructed according to the tastes of the Roundheads, according to the ways of the hopelessly undemanding dogmatists in their new skin and their renewed spirit of vulgarity. It is true that the diplomatic excrement of the New Yugoslavia, the Great Sovietski Soiuz or Bulgaria are instantly recognizable against the cultivated representatives of France or the eccentric representatives of England. However, the domineering tone, the familiar breath is not blown into the corridors of the Palais du Luxembourg by Europeans but by the boorish Russians and the Americans, very different from the Russians in demeanour but strikingly similar in their vulgarity. The greyness of Soviet Communists at some point begins to irresistibly remind me of the garish conspicuousness of the Yankees. With the mandatory ties around their necks, the Russian and Yugoslav dimwits walk around the Palais de Luxembourg as if awaiting execution by hanging. Afraid of people, ignorant of other languages, they communicate with hand gestures (like baboons), if at all, and move everywhere in packs, the only way they feel safe.

The Americans, on the other hand, are strolling around the luxurious Palais like the Yankee at the court of King Arthur. The world is theirs. There are no more Knights of the Round Table, no more knighthood. The world, my dear Jovan, has been conquered by two dangerously uncivil peoples – the Russians and the Americans.

153

Last night, Brana managed to find tickets for the Vieux-Colombier where a contemporary play is currently showing – *Huis Clos* by Jean-Paul Sartre. The piece is very unusual and not quite comprehensible; it takes place in hell, which is a salon decorated in the Second Empire style. I think that the author's thesis is that others, the mere existence of others turns one's life into a nightmare, hell: "Ah! Quelle plaisanterie. Pas besoin de gril: l'enfer, c'est les autres" – says Sartre's hero, reading my own thoughts and emotions.

The other thesis of this writer/philosopher is dangerous, destructive. It frightened me. It still haunts my mind. If I understood the play correctly, that Sartre fellow claims that man is nothing other than what he has done, that he can never surpass his actions, that indeed, he doesn't exist outside of them: "Seuls les actes décident de ce qu'on a voulu. Tu n'es rien d'autre que ta vie."

Isn't that idea terrifying, Jovan? If man is what he has done, what are you then, Jovan? What am I? What is Estelle Choffard, Brana's acquaintance who got us the tickets, now a hat checker in the Vieux-Colombier, with the salary of a street cleaner, otherwise the widow of a Sorbonne professor who died as a maquis in the resistance? Madame Estelle, herself an expert in seventeenth-century French literature, is now checking hats and coats for a living. Is she then the sum of her actions? Or is she, are we, what we don't do but are?

No, Jovan. Completed banalities cannot possibly determine your essence or mine. The others are hell, but we are not devils, regardless of our doing. We, dear Jovan, are angels without a country, for heaven exists no more, the world exists no more.

And so, dear Jovan, now, I shall uncover to you, my dearest Jovan, a truth about that world, a realization which strikes me as fatal whenever I start believing that it is final, a truth you will not like though you must hear it:

THIS IS A WORLD WHICH KRSMANS WILL ENTER WITH EASE, WHILE WE MUST ENTER IT WITH THEM OR NOT AT ALL.

There, I said it.

You see, dear Jovan, my dear little one, that is what I never managed to tell you in sufficiently understandable terms, possibly because prior to my Paris trip, I was secretly hoping that the Communist invasion would be stopped at the ramparts of the western world, that the *antemurale civilitatis*, like the Christian bulwark in Turkish times, would stretch along our borders, but that one could cross that bulwark into a world of better customs and cultivated habits, a world that might at least resemble if not be identical to ours, which shielded us from the worst humiliations while it still existed.

It's gone. That world has disappeared, Jovan. We have been sentenced to Krsman's kind by a final verdict. I am not telling you this to justify myself nor am I blaming you for anything. Everything now is as it is and evidently, as it was bound to be. That which my heart suspected with deadly fear – even when I viciously opposed you in our drunken brawls with no beginning, no purpose and no result; even when, desperate in my heart but decisive in my actions, I allowed Krsman to approach our preserve as the saviour of the battered remains of our former independence – is now entering my consciousness as a tragic inevitability, right here in vulgarized Paris.

I know what I am talking about, Jovan.

I passed through *antemurale civilitatis* and entered a wasteland.

The new masters of the world speak Russian and American, while we, dear Jovan, must either silence our voices or learn those languages.

From one of the translators of the Soviet delegation, I heard the proverb:

"Cheloviek padlietz ka vsemu privikaet". (Man is a wretch who will get used to anything.)

Let that be the first sentence I have learned of the language the new world speaks.

No signature. No date. Five sheets of graph paper. Written in green ink on both sides of the sheet. The handwriting is tiny, firm, stubborn, but – *très féminin*. I can easily imagine the woman who writes like this. That woman resembles Kojović's description of my grandmother Jelena.

So there. That's why I was all set for putting it into the book.

"Oh, yeah?" This is what I said when Bonehead remarked that it "brought chaos to the storyline", that it didn't "progress the action". Who's the drama student in this house?

Yes, I know. Bonehead is right – it's dateless, unmailed, doesn't fit the course of other events. This letter doesn't fill in the gaps in the story of my granny's love-life so much as it deepens them. But what can you do? Bonehead and I agreed at the very beginning that there would only be as much story in this book as is available. Where there's no story, there's a gap. We're not going to try filling the gap. We'll leave it as it is. Case closed. We don't have that right. Of course, I could make up everything that's missing from the Inventarium Helenae, everything that even Kojović doesn't know, everything we couldn't dig up in our "research", but I'm not going to. We don't have the authority, 'cause we're not the authors. Plain and simple. We're just putting together what is, showing what those people were doing. No secrets. No bullshit. That's not our business. We are the presenters, the literary directors if you like. And that means: we can't direct what doesn't exist.

And since Jelena's letter exists, the reader can stick it into the plot whichever way he feels is right. What I don't know, I can't explain to others.

There.

"D'you agree?" I ask Bonehead.

"I do," he says.

Bonehead would agree anyway (he is genetically unfit to argue), but that Tuesday, when we were supposedly arguing about Jelena's letter, was extra special. He had no intention of getting angry because I'd promised we would attend the Saint Jovan's Day celebration (the biggest Orthodox feast in Moslavina) singing, eating and drinking ourselves to death with Bonehead's wild Orthodox compatriots. I knew it would be unbearable, but I just couldn't say no. He looks at me with those Bambi eyes – and I tell you – a militant Catholic would succumb to the magic of those eyes, to say nothing of me – some fuckin' Orthodox Christian and Bonehead devotee!

XI

Bonehead scarpered. Fucking arsehole.

I woke up yesterday morning.

I touched the pillow next to me.

No Bonehead.

I guess I could have assumed for a second that he was having a piss, making coffee, reading the paper or whatever. Somehow, though, I knew immediately: Bonehead had gone to number 3 Terazije Street.

I leapt from my bed.

Manically awake.

I have to say: I saw it coming. As soon as our Croat brothers seized that bridge, as soon as the papers started delivering their spiel about the superiority of the Ustašhe murderers and the withdrawal of the celestial fartheads – I knew: Bonehead won't resist this one. While his team was winning, there was still a chance. Now that they're losing, not a chance in hell.

I threw my clothes on and ran out. I stormed into 3 Terazije Street. "Volunteer Registration – Second Floor". Lift – in full working condition. As I was about to step in, the door opened and out came Bonehead.

I didn't say a word. He didn't say a word. We left the building and walked home, hand in hand, like some fucking modern-day Hansel and Gretel. We walked and stared at our feet in silence. He humbled. Me mad as a dog. I had the urge to knock someone's teeth out. When we got to the park, I said:

"When are you leaving?"

"Today," he said.

My legs turned to jelly. I plopped down on a bench. Lucky it was there, 'cause I'd have fallen right on my backside. Bambi sat down too, right next to me. Guiltridden. He had the look of a kid who'd shat in his pants and knew he had done something really bad.

"I had to, Jela," he said.

I collected myself. I focused all my energy on appearing sweet.

"You gotta do what you gotta do," I replied, quoting some giant of Serbian political theory. Rumour has it that humour is a better antidote than moaning. So I'm trying it out.

"Are you angry with me, Jela?"

"I'm not, sweetheart," I said and kissed him on the cheek. "Let's go home, you goose."

I was boiling inside. I couldn't tell if I was furious or completely in the dumps.

While we waited for the light in Nemanjina Street, he said:

"Will you finish the book while I'm gone?"

"Fuck the book."

"Don't say that, Jela. I'd like you to finish it. There ain't much left. The only thing left in the Inventarium Helenae is Krsman's letter."

"Which we don't understand."

"We don't, you're right, but you said you'd take it to Kojović. Maybe he can work it out."

I'm listening and thinking: this is really fucked up. What sodding book? Who the fuck are Vrcalov, Krsman and the rest of them anyway? They mean nothing to me! Am I nuts?!

Still, all that talk about the book somehow grounded me, I suppose. The moron that I am, I thought for a millisecond: maybe all is not lost. We have five hours. The contingent of fresh Serbian beef isn't leaving until 4 p.m.

"Are you travelling by refrigerator trucks?" I asked.

"No. Military buses," Bonehead said meekly.

"Where to?"

"I ain't really sure what plan they got for us. First, they said we're going to some training camp, somewhere around Bosanski Petrovac, but that ain't me, I'm pretty sure – I'm a trained artillery man."

This is where I launched my offensive. I fashioned my deep throat wailing after the example of rape and ethnic cleansing victims I saw on TV.

"What's the matter with you, woman!" Bonehead yelled back in shock. The poor guy didn't recognize me.

"I don't care if you have a Ph.D in artillery studies, dickhead! Do you hear me?! You'll go and you'll get trained like the rest of them! I'll immolate myself right here in fucking central Belgrade! I'll burn myself like a Indian widow, I give you my word on that!"

The screaming proved effective – Bonehead promised. I felt better for a few minutes. I hoped that while he was training, the rest of the necrophiles would kill themselves at will and by the time Bonehead got to the front, there'd be no one left to kill him.

Then I realized it was a stupid idea. They'll fight this war as long as there's live cattle to spare. That's the way of the world. I've read Freud's letter to Einstein. I read the papers. No fucking way. That stuff is as clear as day.

Suddenly, I felt like shit.

Worse than shit.

We got home. Bonehead roamed around the room, packing. Silently. Secretly, every now and again, he looked from the corner of his eye.

Once he mumbled more to himself:

"Like two thieves caught in the act." I pretended not to hear. Around 1:30 p.m., hoarse from my silence strike, I asked in my Tom Waits-esque voice:

"How will you go to the front without long underwear?"

"I'll get them from the army."

That was the extent of our conversation.

I didn't know what else I could possibly: a) say b) do, so I sat in the middle of the room, sprawled out on the sofa like a fat cow, following Bonehead with my eyes like a tennis ball in a match.

When he finished packing, he asked:

"Would you like some waffles?"

I didn't answer.

So he made waffles.

159

We ate the waffles, while they, in Scumbag's words, ate away at us.

Bonehead shrank with guilt; at this point, he was beginning to look like the hunchback of Notre-Dame.

After lunch he gathered courage: he sat down on the sofa and threw his arm around me.

I took his arm off my shoulder. That second.

"You're angry with me, aren't you?"

No answer from me.

Crushed, he washed the dishes. He also vacuumed and cleared up the room, knowing that from then on, no one would ever bother with it. But the real reason he did it was something else: in the infra-red silence I radiated (I could have set a couple of rooms on fire), he needed to do something, anything, since he couldn't say a word – it was obvious I'd turned into a fucking time bomb.

At 3:15 p.m., he put on his coat. He threw his backpack on his shoulder. Ready for departure.

I was reading a magazine.

"Are you gonna see me off to the bus, then?" he asked, already standing by the door.

I didn't raise my eyes from the page:

"No," I said.

Didn't budge.

"Are you gonna kiss me at least?" he asked.

For a second, I raised my eyes to look at him. His eyes were swollen with tears. I went back to reading the magazine. I didn't look again. And I said, like the total fucking arsehole that I am, I said:

"No."

Then he left. Untouched, unkissed.

I went on a drinking binge. Alone. Finished a whole bottle of brandy.

I woke up sometime around midnight. My head was about twice the size of my body. My mouth stank worse than an ashtray. Everything seemed mad. I thought to myself, in all seriousness:

"What if I just topped myself right now?"

Instead, I went to the kitchen and made myself an omelette with three eggs. Had a beer. Fell asleep, again.

In the morning, I had a shower. It lasted for at least forty minutes.

I took out the Inventarium Helenae, just to occupy myself with something.

I read Krsman's letter once more:

The handwriting's kind of primitive, though luckily, legible – every letter's clear as a bell. The content on the other hand, what can I say – total fucking nonsense. Like he couldn't even approximately express his thoughts. It starts off like this:

"Well it aint goin be the same no more! You can't have your way and I aint gonna shout no more. Enuf is enuf. Where d'you see peoples screwing like they's strangers!"

That I still understand, more or less, but then it gets totally absurd:

"If I'm guilty, I'm goin to testify for you and for the court. No willy nelly. It's true, I'm a country boy. So what Stavra didn't hold me at the baptism. But it aint me, I swear on me dead mother. This I want say something to you, I can do beter. I spent enuf time coverin you. You got to wake up, woman, look around you. Everybody want somethin and maybe you aint even good enuf. Peoples is afraid of me I make theyr blood run cold and you fuck around with me. Mayby its for the best that you leave me alone. Everythin around you's like rotten wood everything you touch you turn to rot woman! You can cry til tomorow but I ain't goin to get kicked around. This much I can tell you enuf is enuf. You can't tell me what to do I am a colonel. leftenent-colonel Krsman Jakšić."

A five-year-old's words. Totally incomprehensible. No date. Since I found it in Jelena's bag, I worked out it was addressed to her.

And then I ask myself: What the fuck is up anyway? Do I really care about Krsman and his nonsensical bullshit?! His sexual excursions with Jelena matter to me as much as the sex drive of Galapagos turtles! I don't give a damn who fathered Scumbag and I don't give three shits who had the brilliant idea to make me!

So I went ballistic again. With me, anger isn't just plain anger; it's a sort of itch, like an unbearable itch, I can't describe it. When I was little, I bit my dog Rufus on the leg. He wouldn't eat ice cream. That's what I mean: when I'm this angry, I need to bite. The problem is – I had nothing to bite.

I roamed around the house like a sow on heat. I washed my hair. As soon as it dried, I washed it again. Nothing to bite – that's what I mean. In the afternoon, after a long day like that, I dialled Kojović's number.

The old man had caught the flu. His voice was so weak I could barely hear him.

"Have you called an ambulance?" I asked.

They've already come and gone, he said. The doctor didn't even take off her coat. Barely sat down for a split second. Drink plenty of fluids, take aspirin, tralala. See you when you're better.

So then I called Birdy. His girlfriend Goca just finished medicine – maybe she'll know. Goca came to see the old bloke. Definitely not pneumonia, she said. He should rest, not lying down but sitting. And I should cook up a batch of strong beef broth for him.

When Goca left, I admitted to Kojović that I didn't know how to.

"That's all right," he said, "I do."

I went down to Alonso's shop. In my "household", Bonehead was the shopper till yesterday, so I had no clue what costs what. Imagine my delight at finding out that a pound of steak (bone included) costs two hundred billion! Pretty fucking demented.

"Son, you must be insane," I said to the butcher.

"Son? You're calling me son? I'm twice yer age, woman. I could be yer father," the butcher said to me.

"Cool it, Dad," I said and grabbed the hunk of meat.

We made the soup through a joint effort, the old geezer and me. His ideas, my horsepower. The soup turned out pretty much like the real stuff. Old Fiacre had a sip, then said:

"I hate to sound sentimental, Miss Jelena, but I must say: I find your attention and care touching. I can't remember the last time someone cooked soup for an old bachelor like me."

I feel myself turning into a pile of mush, I can't help it suddenly.

I'm on the verge of snivelling like some stupid cow. To bring things back to normal, I hand Kojović Krsman's letter to him.

"Does this mean anything to you? Means zilch to Bogdan and me."

I heard myself saying "Bogdan" and I almost got the shivers. I have no idea why I called him that, even less of an idea why I suddenly felt cosy calling him by his name. But I did. I later worked out why: Hearing his name and surname somehow reassured me that he existed, somewhere, if not here. Someone, somewhere was calling his name off a list: "Bogdan Bilogorac!" And he was responding: "Here!"

Fuckin' a. As my man Turber would say: "A dog needs very little to be happy."

The old man took his time with the letter. Read it once. Read it again. Finally, he said:

"How did you find this letter?"

Here, for the first time, I told him about the Inventarium Helenae. I also told him (finally) that we're making a book.

"A book? Very nice, very nice. And will there be room for my claptrap in this book?"

"'Course. Without your help, there'd be no book at all –" (I remembered the words I used in the acknowledgment. I was joking – like an automatic reflex or whatever. In fact, everything seemed completely insane – the joking and the non-joking aspects.)

"Well, if you ask me, I would say . . ." Kojović was about to start his spiel but I interrupted him:

"Let me just turn on the tape recorder."

"Before taking this to your publisher, Miss Jelena, would you mind lending me the transcriptions of my words? I would like to edit them a little."

"Of course I don't mind. I'll bring them over."

The tape recorder's on; the end's around the corner.

OLD MAN KOJOVIĆ (3)

OLD FIACRE:

What can I say, Miss Jelena. Judging from this letter, one would think that maybe they were lovers after all. I admit that you have won our bet, if you care much for that, though I must take this opportunity to reprimand you: you are a little weasel, Miss Jelena. Playing with the mind of an old man like that! You knew all along about the contents of the Inventarium, and not a word of it to me! Oh well. I shouldn't complain: *Senum consilia, iuventum robur.*

ME:

I wanted your testimony to be 100 per cent authentic wool. No synthetic materials added, you know what I mean? It's not a question of anything else, I promise.

OLD FIACRE:

Perhaps you're right – perhaps I played a more useful role by guessing, feeling my way through the dark aspects of the young Arandjelovićs' bloody romance. Yet, in spite of your data, you see, I still have trouble believing that Krsman and Jelena were lovers. Try as I may, I simply cannot imagine such an impossibility. Porcelain-skinned Jelena and goat-herding shepherd Krsman – in bed! The baker-colonel who killed a thousand men and seduced a thousand women in bed with the Belgrade princess. Then again, how should I know? Those were turbulent times. Like today, a dark era of ruin-ation. And in such an era, all is possible; even the worst becomes a likelihood.

Kojović paused to think. His jaw started moving up and down, like he was chewing on something. All of a sudden, he looked really old, withered. Pretty hard to believe that this is the same old polished dandy I met in "The Blue Rider". I looked at him, and I suddenly had this image of an old man sleeping on a park bench, covered with news-papers, with a plastic bag under his head. I felt really sorry for the old geezer. So I didn't rush him. He'll pick up when he's ready. And eventually:

OLD FIACRE:

Still, you see, there is a cosmic justice mightier than evil times. Hubris is a real crossing, you see, the crossing of a real line. The rape of borders laid down by the gods to surround human action. Man can't have it all, it's that simple. I don't know if you share my opinion, Miss Jelena, though whatever you may think, the gods exist. Yes, yes, one of those rare wonders one must never doubt. Perhaps the gods are in Olympus, perhaps they are within us, within our honest thoughts, perhaps they are in a flower – where Lord Tennyson sought them. Wherever they may be they exist. They must exist, Miss Jelena . . .

ME:

No objection.

I'm trying to manoeuvre us out of this rhetorical mess, but the old guy ain't giving up.

OLD FIACRE:

Imagine a world without gods. Imagine a world populated only by people! It would be an unbearable place in which the human encroachment of boundaries drawn by divine hands, an encroachment on the scale of Krsman and Lena's love meddling, even such an encroachment would pass unpunished. As you know, it didn't. The gods intervened, proving once again that they do exist!

ME:

It seems that they also erased all traces of their intervention. The gods, I mean. I'm telling you, Mr Kojović, Bogdan (again, the tranquillizing effect of that word) and I have literally ploughed through the *Borba* and the *Politika* for the months of March and April 1945, and not a word about that murder! And not just murder: murder and suicide, which is an even bigger catch. It just doesn't make any sense. I mean, we've got a jewel here. The heart of every reporter beats faster at such an opportunity. And it's not like Joe Nobody from Pratt Street was murdered, you know? It was Krsman Jakšić, the OZNA lieutenant colonel, the Communist hair-raising demi-god.

OLD FIACRE:

A hair-raising Communist who *thought* he was a demi-god.

ME:

Is it possible that not a single newspaper, I mean not one, printed a word about it?! Do you have a theory? Bogdan and I are clueless.

OLD FIACRE:

No theory is necessary, Miss Jelena, because there is an explanation. A logical concise explanation that resides in the period we are discussing. I must warn you again that words, like people, age on the inside, die and are born anew, identical in shape but carrying new meanings with their changed molecular structures. Hence, the current connotation of the term "the press" cannot successfully explain the *Politika* and the *Borba* of the tempestuous Belgrade 1945. Those were called newspapers, then as now, but the newspapers which you read are a different breed altogether. Newspapers existed as mediums for the publication of their angular Leninist words of wisdom, their Bolshevik evangelism. The *Borba* and *Politika* of those days are most comparable (even though it's not a perfect correlation, naturally), to today's *Official Messenger* in the following sense: you certainly wouldn't expect the *Official Messenger* to report on a spectacular shooting in a neighbourhood bar, now would you? Of course not! In the same vein, one cannot expect the *Borba* of 1945 to report on a murder and a suicide. Nothing private, nothing individual, nothing which could be reduced to a name and a surname ever entered that newspaper. In the newpapers, the individual did not exist. For example, not a single detail concerning Tito's private life was published in the papers for years. One knew that he had grown up in the village of Kumrovec, nothing more. Who his father was, if he had any siblings, whether he was married or not – those remained secrets. The papers reported in infinitesimal detail about his presence at congressional sessions and hearings, of course, but nothing personal. Thus, and I know that you cannot fully grasp such an idea, printing that some Jovan killed some Krsman and himself out of jealous rage would be on a par with blasphemy, equal to printing obscene jokes in the Vatican newspaper – the *Osservatore Romano*, for example. The *Borba* and the *Politika* of 1945 could not conceive of the existence of hardheaded individuals living their lives against what the newspapers dictated; they could not conceive of why people so obstinately do as they wish rather than doing what the newspapers indoctrinate them with. Private lives, the vileness of betrayal, the stinking, decaying remnants of the past. It's commendable to love one's fatherland and reprehensible to love one's hometown; one must worship Tito and be indifferent to one's own father; it's proper to be concerned with the proletariat and the youth, but not with one's friends and children.

To say nothing at all about lovers or sweethearts! In conclusion: it's worthy of praise to kill for Socialism, the great leader and the working class, but killing for a woman – good heavens, no! *Apage Satanas*. Let us conceal the stain with silence.

ME:

Yeah. I get it. But you see, Bogdan thought they wanted to hush up the whole scandal. You know – embarrassment to OZNA, that sort of thing.

OLD FIACRE:

Oh that too, certainly. Had he nobly lost his life chasing "class enemies" around town, there'd be a nineteen-gun salute. There'd be speeches by co-servicemen, and In Memoriams on the editorial page. But which Communist parting words does one write in honour of a skirt-chaser killed by a jealous rival? That merely strengthened their editorial adherence to principle: jealousy is prohibited because not even romantic passion is recommended. That which is prohibited, from the editorial point of view, simply does not exist. Thus, no murder or suicide took place at all. Logical, you must admit.

ME:

Well, Mr Kojović, logical maybe, but our book is about murders and suicide and runs mostly on romantic passion. So, I must kindly ask you on behalf of Mr Bilogorac and myself, to slowly, leisurely, as only you and Roger Martin du Klenak know how, tell me everything you know about the murder. We've reached the end of the book. There's about one million gaps in it already, but this one would be humungous. Without the murder, the title of the book wouldn't make any sense, right? A proper "*scène à faire*", as Archer would say. So, Mr Kojović, let's get the bugger finished.

HOW JOVAN KILLED KRSMAN AND HIMSELF

OLD FIACRE:

Gladly, Miss Jelena, gladly. Though you'll see, I don't know much more than you do or than what is common knowledge.

Ergo, in the briefest possible terms:

Everything took place in their flat. I say "flat" because as you know, their house in Krunska Street was confiscated and inhabited by Communist trash. Jelena and Jovan were left with two rooms with a back entrance and the servants' toilet – that's what I'm calling a "flat". That's where the drama was concluded.

Krsman was having lunch in Krunska Street. He had hung his belt and his revolver on the coat hook in the corridor. At one point during lunch, Jovan got up without any explanation. He went to the corridor, removed the revolver from the lieutenant colonel's holster, returned to the room and shot Krsman five times. He then shot himself in the mouth with the remaining bullet.

The investigation didn't establish much beyond these vague and obvious facts. It didn't establish much, it seemed to me, not because it was impossible to know, but rather because the investigators weren't really interested in the case. I remember that there was a sort of visible dispassion to their whole approach, a sort of disgust at having to investigate a case with no political background. During our first conversation, I described the dusty official who interrogated me about the murder. When I said that I didn't know anything about Jovan's and Jelena's behaviour during the occupation, my statement momentarily became worthless to him in every respect. They were after national traitors, political enemies. They didn't take any interest in criminals, murderers, thieves, unless they were also "class enemies". Besides, the semblance of a judicial proceedings is only the last recourse, so that anything, even seemingly legal, would precede the murder *they* will perform regardless of the results of the investigation and the strength of the defence's argument. From their perspective then, it must have seemed rather stupid to bring charges against a perpetrator who had taken his own life as well. "Formalism". It was pointless "formalism" for them – and formalism, you know, is one of the most revealing words from their blasphemous vocabulary. A simple waste of time, unworthy of the efficient Communist police. To paraphrase a sentence from Krsman's letter: "They make your blood run cold". Heavens, we can't expect them to waste time with childish court proceedings, those human bastions of power and might!

It is with such a sentiment that the dusty interrogator conducted this case. So as not to appear to be interrupting the interrogation too abruptly, he asked about Jelena, you remember – "Does she sleep around?", but he didn't bother waiting for my reply to his vulgar, basely constructed suggestion, because he wasn't really interested in what was happening inside the love triangle (that is, assuming you're right and assuming that it was a love triangle).

Jelena's hearing was similar. Can you imagine? The testimony of the crucial witness, the only witness to this horrific event. The dusty interrogator asked her the same question, though in a somewhat more refined manner than he had asked me:

"Did you have a sexual relationship with your brother Jovan?"

Jelena shot straight from the hip:

"And did you sleep with your mother Nelly?"

This response was so unexpected, that the Communist official lost his cool. He didn't immediately insult her and responded rather foolishly:

"My mother's name isn't Nelly," to which Jelena replied:

"Well, Jovan isn't my brother either."

This, however, was the end of Jelena's arrogance. He slapped her and called her a "bourgeois bitch" – please pardon the expression, Miss Jelena. The sentence which concludes that part of the record remains etched in my memory, perhaps because of its silly judicial triteness:

"The interrogation is temporarily suspended as the witness has started to sob."

ME:

And as to whether with her brother-nonbrother, with Krsman – I mean, did Jelena really tell you nothing about who, where, when, why and that sort of thing?

OLD FIACRE:

Very little. How little – judge for yourself. I'll tell you everything I remember, everything that could, in my opinion, assist you in filling the "narrative gaps" as you have called them, in your praiseworthy book.

Jelena called me around three o'clock on a Sunday, waking me up from my afternoon doze. Her voice was colourless, drained, unnaturally monotonous. It occurs to me that one could compare it to the automatic answering services of large businesses. That's right – only now does it cross my mind! Ever since answering machines became fashionable, I have been asking myself why I get shivers down my spine every time I speak into them, as if I were talking to non-beings. Only now do I realize that after all these years, the ghostlike indifference of answering-machine voices reminds me of Jelena's voice on that Sunday afternoon:

"Brana, Jovan killed Krsman," she said.

"How?" I asked fatuously. Having been awakened from my sleep I was still unable to grasp the incredible news.

"Shot him. Please come over," she said and hung up, while I, flabbergasted, uttered my belated reply into the dead receiver:

"I'm coming."

As you can see, Miss Jelena, it's most interesting (though I would be capable of thinking about this only much later) that Jelena didn't mention a word about Jovan's suicide when she called. Think about what that might have meant. Perhaps the bizarre omission was the result of a state of psychological shock. In other words, in Jelena's perturbed consciousness the announcement that Krsman had been shot possibly contained an implied, albeit unspoken flip side of the same abomination – Jovan's suicide. This most likely explains Jelena's omission at the time.

However, after much deliberation, it seems unadvisable to me to entirely reject the possibility that Krsman's murder stood above Jovan's suicide in Jelena's disturbed hierarchy. Naturally, if one accepts this possibility, one must also examine the opposite: perhaps Jelena's defence mechanism could grapple with the fact that Krsman was dead, that Jovan had committed the murder, but not with the unbearable truth of her brother's suicide.

Much guesswork, little certainty, I know. But why not guess, Miss Jelena? Guesswork has never killed anyone. Yet, unsubstantiated verdicts have sent millions to their deaths.

ME (impolitely):

Let's return to the story, shall we?

OLD FIACRE (obediently, uninsultedly):

Let us return to the story. Right. Let us return to the story. You must forgive me – *Senectus est natura loquacior*. Very well then. When I arrived at the house in Krunska Street, I was astounded by the incredibly idyllic tableau in the front garden. I was expecting the police, sirens, blood. Instead I had stumbled upon an image from a winter's tale: a crowd of little people, teeny little kids, all bundled up and ready to face the day. Wrapped in their many layers they looked like a gang of dumpy little cubs – flushed, boisterous, exhilarated, divided into two camps waging a fierce battle with wet, early March snowballs. There was a whole crowd of them – ten, maybe even twenty. The yard teemed with them, the air teemed with snowballs, clean white snowballs flying in all directions. One of the snowballs struck me in the back, but charmed as I was by the heavenly tableau, I was virtually convinced at that instant that the terrible news I had heard over the telephone had to be some great though easily explainable mistake.

Unfortunately, that wasn't the case. A bewhiskered ogre opened the door. He was from the court, or from the police, I didn't know exactly. At any rate, he was one of the four people pacing around the apartment, conducting the inspection and writing a report on the event. Following a series of dispassionate, apathetic questions, he asked:

"D'she speak to you on the telephone?"

"Yes."

He stared at his pad, reading with difficulty:

"Branko Kojović. That's you, eh?"

"Yes."

"Are you a relative?"

"Yes."

"All right. Step in." The giant let me through.

For a moment, I stood at the door. Though informed about the murder, I was entirely unprepared for the sight before me:

In the middle of the room stood the dining table, covered with dirty dishes and food scraps. To the left of the table (left from my perspective), by the legs, bundled into a ball, as if suffering from a convulsion, in a pool of deep red blood which had not yet dried, lay Krsman. The chair, I assumed it was the one he had been sitting on, was turned over, thus concealing Krsman's head from my view. The left wall, the wall behind Krsman's body was sprayed with blood.

Very near the door where I stood, a mere two feet from the tips of my shoes, lay Jovan's outstretched body. One couldn't tell it was him by looking at his face – the head and the face, the vile and amorphous glob of blood, brain tissue, skull and hair resembled the remains of a run-over dog on the road. The mass lay in a blotch of blood, different from Krsman's. It was dark, soaking into the wine-coloured rug.

To the side, in an exquisitely selected viewing spot, sufficiently removed so as to encompass the entire tableau with one look, was Jelena, feverishly huddling against the green armchair. Wakefully, tensely, with great ardour I would say, she observed the field of blood before her. Huddled snugly in her chair, she was all eyes. She reminded me of a spectator in the theatre whose attention was singlemindedly committed to the action onstage.

I don't know if it happened just so, but I do know that this is how I remember it. And not only that. I remember something else – something even more bizarre than the expression of spectatorial curiosity on Jelena's face, something which cannot be easily explained, yet it has been needling me for half a century now, even though it's been inconsequential. It's entirely impossible for Jelena's armchair to have been elevated from the floor, resting upon some sort of pedestal, podium, rostrum. I don't know what that was, what that could have been, but I can't help it – I seem to remember seeing Jelena on some sort of elevation. I know, I know – pedestal or no pedestal, what does that change in the horrific order of things? The curious thing however is that I had actually noticed an elevation in a place where there were plenty of horrors to occupy one's attention.

And although everything in that inconceivable scene was repulsive, nothing shocked me so – not the blood on the wall, not the puddle on the floor, not the blasted head and torso of the boy I had known and loved from the cradle – as seeing Jelena, elevated upon her pedestal, observing the horror so unyieldingly, with such voyeur-like devotion! I don't quite know why I found the unnatural discordance between the butcherly sight and the heedless curiosity on Jelena's face so terrifying. I remember, however, that in that moment, I irrevocably lined up according to their degree of urgency those things which needed to be done, and following that order the most pressing of all was to remove the sight from Jelena's eyes, or to avert Jelena's eyes from the sight, which amounts to the same. Don't ask me how, despite my agitation I still managed to be cold-bloodedly certain that this order, coming from someone calm and superior, was unquestionable. Not even today am I capable of telling you why I deemed it so important to separate the scene of butchery and Jelena in their voyeur-exhibitionist, eroticized exchange. All I can say is that my first impulse was to leap to the armchair on the pedestal (which certainly could not have been there), and cover Jelena's eyes with my hand.

At the moment when my leg had already extended in that direction, I realized that the way to the armchair led across Jovan's body, that I had to cross it in order to reach my destination, cross it like a rotten trunk on a forest road or a disgusting lump of dog flesh and fur on the street. I wanted to do it, but my legs, independent of my intention, stood still, stiff as two rods held in place by a divine string of some sort. The conflict between two opposite yet equally strong impulses held me at a dynamic zero point, in a state of painful immobility, as if I had been magically petrified. I don't know how long I would have stood by the door, had a bewhiskered Montenegrin not so much as removed me from there.

"Move aside, Comrade," he said, pushing me out of his way to make room for a duo of undertakers waiting behind me with a stretcher.

When they threw Jovan's body on to the stretcher, unfazed by the pieces of blasted head and doughy mass remaining on the floor, and when they reached the door, Jelena rose and followed. She placed her arm under mine. We walked behind the stretchers like a mourning family in a funeral procession.

There was nobody left in the front yard when we came out. Perhaps they had stopped playing of their own accord but it's more likely that they had been chased away. Mind you, in those times, children were rather accustomed to cadavers. Between the spring of '41 and the autumn of '44, they probably had to jump over dead bodies in streets and entrance ways rather often.

They dumped Jovan's body into an uncovered Russian truck by turning the stretcher over and simply dropping it flat. Jelena and I stood by. Jelena glared at the cobblestone before her feet. Right after that, they took out Krsman and dumped him beside Jovan. As the driver was lifting and locking the back gate, I asked the bewhiskered Montenegrin whom I saw climb on to the front seat:

"Where are you taking them?"

"To the morgue."

"With your permission, sir, we would like to bury Jovan in our family grave at the New Cemetery," I said, gathering the last scattered remnants of practicality I had left.

"OK. You bury Jovan," the ogre complied.

Then, in that characteristic way of hers, Jelena added without a hint of tentativeness, as if it were a verdict, the closing words of a magistrate:

"We shall also bury Krsman Jakšić."

The ogre stopped instantaneously, with one leg on the rung of the truck and the other on the ground. As he climbed to his seat, he remarked between breaths:

"That's not gonna be possible, m'fraid. The army will bury the lieutenant colonel."

And so it did.

The old guy paused, lost in his thoughts. Again, he started chewing on something non-existent. Again, he looked like some homeless bloke on a park bench. This went on for a while, so I asked:

ME:

Are you tired?

OLD FIACRE (startled):

No. Not really. I'm just a little frail. Not tired.

ME:

Shall I make you some tea? That much I can do.

OLD FIACRE:

If you don't mind. I would be most grateful.

* * *

174

So I made tea. While I waited for the water to boil, I yelled out a question – a stupid question, pretty crude too, but it came to mind:

ME:

Who cleaned the room? I mean, who washed off the blood, picked up the pieces and all that?

OLD FIACRE:

Believe me, I don't know. I must have forgotten. We must have hired someone to do it. I know that Jelena didn't. In fact, not only did she not wash the blood or pick up the pieces – she never stepped into 24 Krunska Street again. When the truck departed, she informed me that she would never go back to that flat. She didn't explain why and I didn't ask questions, naturally. She asked me to go in and bring her astrakhan fur, muff and hat and take her to the old Nerandzics, to Grandpa Petar and Grandma Dušanka, who lived on Birćaninova Street. She lived with them until her departure for the TB Sanatorinmat Golnik, where she died, in '49.

ME:

In '50.

OLD FIACRE:

In '50? It's possible. One forgets these things. I was sure it was '49. The old Nerandzics raised Jelena's daughter, your mother Annabella. Do you remember them?

ME:

No. They died before I was born. But I know the apartment in Birćaninova Street. I still live there.

OLD FIACRE:

Right, right. Of course. I know it was in Birćaninova, though I do not remember the building or the apartment itself. Was it spacious?

ME:

One bedroom. Big enough for Bogdan and myself.

OLD FIACRE:

Ah! I didn't get the chance to ask and you never mentioned it: where is Mr Bogdan?

ME:

At the front.

*   *   *

Kojović dropped the cup into the saucer. The porcelain and the teaspoon made a clanking sound. He stared at me. In silence. I realized the old geezer had worked things out for himself. (Before, I wasn't sure if he knew about Bonehead and me. The man's too polite – you can never tell what he's thinking.) Then, he sat up in his bed. He leaned towards me and put his hand on mine.

OLD FIACRE:

I know how you feel, Jelena (no "Miss" for the first time) – I know how you feel, Jelena. But not everything is as black as it surely appears to be. Men go to war and they return from war. I know what I'm talking about, believe me, this one is my third.

"Let's not . . . about that," I said. Why waste words on the unwordable?

So, that's the book.

It is as it is.

I just have to give Kojović his blabber so he can edit it, and then Djuradj can do whatever he wants with the love-life of Grandma Jelena.

What a sodding waste of time.

But I promised. I promised Bogdan.

NOTE FROM THE EDITOR

HOMAGE TO THE AUTHOR OF
PREMEDITATED MURDER

My name is Djuradj Djurić and I am the Belgrade correspondent of Reuters. I am not writing this note in the capacity of a reporter, however, but as the publisher of *Premeditated Murder* – Jelena Panić's book. Amateur publisher, I might add. *Murder* is my fourth book. The previous three were also books written by my friends.

Why did I decide to add this postscript to Jelena Panić's book?

I believe that the answer lies in *Premeditated Murder* itself. It began as a book about Jelena, Jovan, Krsman and the distant 1945, in the course of its composition it became in great part a book about Bulika, Bogdan and the not so distant 1992.

The story about Jelena, Jovan and Krsman is finished, as finished as it could get. The story of Bulika and Bogdan, however, was interrupted at a moment when their destinies became enveloped in great uncertainties. I deemed it my duty, as publisher, witness and most importantly, as Bulika's friend and Bogdan's acquaintance, to finish *Premeditated Murder* – to the degree, of course, that it is possible to finish the lethal course of self-destruction in this country.

I must immediately say that I harbour no literary aspirations in writing this note. This note is a modest homage to my unusual friend, the brave Jelena Panić, whom several of her friends including myself had the habit of calling (not always endearingly) Bulika, short for bull-terrier. The nickname suited her only partially: Bulika proved on many occasions to have the guts of a fearsome fighter but also a heart softer than cotton wool, if you are indeed capable of imagining these two exclusive substances in one embodiment.

Just two days before receiving the directive from my agency that I would be going to the Knin front, Bulika telephoned me to tell me that her boyfriend, Bogdan Bilogorac, had died on the 27th January. At that time, the date of his death was the only information she could establish with any degree of accuracy. In the Belgrade Bureau of the Presidency of the Serbian Krajina Republic as well as in the representative offices of their military headquarters, Bulika's request to have Bogdan's body brought to Belgrade where she wished to bury it in her family grave (next to Jovan and Jelena, the heroes of the book they had assembled together), was politely but firmly refused. One must add that the reservations of the Krajina authorities were justified: Bogdan is not from Belgrade, and Jelena Panić isn't kin, neither close nor distant. Since they could not transport the body to his native Grubišhno Polje, and since no one from the family had called with the desire to bury him elsewhere, they felt it was best to let him rest in peace where death came his way.

But exactly where death came his way and where he rested in peace, Bulika could not find out from Belgrade, in spite of her efforts. When she telephoned the Information Office of the East Bosnian Corpus in Bjeljina, of which Bogdan was part, she was told that a volunteer by that name had died in transport, having fallen into a snare of Muslim units on the Majevica front, somewhere between the villages Brusnica and Lukavica.

Given that this information did not coincide at all with the information she was given in Belgrade, Bulika asked her colleague from the university – Gaja Simić, a native of Banja Luka and editor of the recently founded periodical *The New Turning Point*, to check on the information from Bijeljina. He quickly established that it was indeed a mistake. A certain Bogdan Belogrlic had died in a road siege between Brusnica and Lukavica as early as the 11th January, before Bogdan Bilogorac had even left Belgrade. Having informed her of this, Gaja advised her to do something which she, extremely shaken by the death of her boyfriend, subsequently related to me as a firm decision:

"I have to go to Obrovac," she said.

178

I begged her not to, because her plan was dangerous, nearly impossible to execute and pointless to boot, but even as I listed the reasons, I realized that the effort was entirely futile. Bulika was extremely shaken and manically obstinate – as only she is capable of being. Someone who knew her less well than I might have overlooked the depth of her despair. But I didn't. Behind the veneer of Bulika's swearwords, curses, behind her crude jargon, I saw a friend driven mad by an irretrievable loss. As it was in her bullterrieresque nature to accept impossibilities with difficulty, she invested all the destructive energy of her acute pain over Bogdan's death into the decision to go ahead with her (unfortunately) completely insane plan.

"You know, mate," she said, lighting one cigarette after another as if entranced, "I saw him off like a dog. I didn't even kiss him. I have to find him. I have to kiss him."

Bulika was a born "loner", as she would say, or an "individualist", as the rest of us might call it. I don't know if she had any friends other than Birdy and myself, and even with the two of us, the friendships weren't ordinary. We saw each other irregularly, and by and large rarely. Sometimes a month or two would pass and we wouldn't even have spoken on the phone. Despite that, however, I knew that Bulika was a person I could rely on more than on anyone else. In every respect. The feeling that there is someone who won't abandon you when you're in trouble, in spite of the personal sacrifice, makes an individual's life stable and develops his capacity for solidarity. Bulika was thus always very important to me, and at the hour of her great misfortune, I knew I had to help her.

When I realized that I couldn't dissuade Bulika from her mad undertaking, the least I could do was to accompany her on her trip and help her out. In the offices of SRNA,* in 8 Mose Pijade Street, we were told that passes for Knin were issued only to accredited reporters. We overcame this obstacle by convincing my agency to hire Jelena as a war photographer. Together with Jeremy Piper – a correspondent from the *Guardian* – and Susan Tarnbull – a freelancer from Chicago – we

*Press agency of the insurgent Serbian Republic of Krajina in Croatia.

departed for Knin on the 7th February. We made the trip in the private Mercedes of Slavko Montenegrin from Benkovac, a man reputed to be the most skilful and most informed guide to worldly-wise seekers of truth and other sensations on the mined corridor Semberija-Bosanska Posavina-Bosanska Krajina-Knin.

Thanks to him and to sheer luck, of course, our trip was spared major complications. Our greatest source of distress was not the militia men standing at control posts, nor any of the drunken patriotic hordes Slavko Montenegrin managed to handle excellently, but the fact that Susan Tarnbull was a strict vegetarian! I am amazed to this day that we got out alive from the ramshackle, bullet-hole-ridden, deserted house near the village of Patkovač, where we had been invited for a meal of roast lamb by a certain overly hospitable character named George. Apart from the fact that his name was George and that he drove a Mitsubishi Land Rover, we knew absolutely nothing about our host. Having met Jeremy Piper somewhere in Bjeljina, he told the correspondent that he worked in Switzerland as a metalsmith and that he periodically took unpaid leave to fight Croats and Muslims in his native Krajina. The inquisitive reporter saw in that the material for a great "story", thus convincing the rest of us, despite our guide Slavko's opposition, to accept the invitation.

We realized soon enough that Slavko's caution was entirely justified. Having drunk a significant amount of brandy while the lamb was turning on the skewer, the angelic George suddenly lost his temper. First, we enraged him because we hadn't consumed enough brandy, and later he was driven absolutely mad by the fact that Susan refused to taste his lamb. When the sworn vegetarian stuck by her decision even after a repeated request, the hospitable George began firing his Kalashnikov as though possessed. We were lucky that his cohabitants restrained him before he actually shot anyone.

Providence was with us when we arrived in Knin as well. Having registered with the police (as legally prescribed) and requested permission for journalistic work, we made the acquaintance of the Minister of Information in the government of RSK, a certain Mr Stojiljkovic, if I remember the name correctly, who promised Bulika that he would procure a permit from the military authorities to transport Bogdan Bilogorac's remains to Belgrade.

Another obstacle was thus overcome.

It turned out, however, that finding the remains of Bulika's Bogdan was a bigger hassle than we ever could have suspected. By all accounts, the 27th January had been a bloody day, ridden with horrific tension, making the memories of soldiers unreliable. The main operation of the RSK army was the counter-offensive on the frontline Smilčić-Kašić-Islam Grčki and many soldiers had died there. Furthermore, on that same day, additional, equally bloody battles were waged on the line Jasenice-Rovanjska, as well as for the dominant peak by the hamlet of Skabranja and for the Lesser and Greater Bobija on the slopes of the Velebit mountain.

It may seem peculiar, but despite Bulika's and my best efforts, we couldn't establish with any certainty in what terrain Bogdan had died. The "Wolves from Wolf Mountain" claimed that Bogdan had been with them and that he had died while approaching Kašić. Their commander however, affirmed that on that day, he had received a new platoon of volunteers and that many of them had died, but he wasn't certain that Bogdan had been among them. A former follower of para-military commander Arkan, who left his leader and joined the volunteers of Lipovača, insulted by his punishment of a beating on the buttocks, claimed that Bogdan had died by his side, as they were trying to conquer the peak above Skabranja. A young woman with a shaved head in the "Saint Sava" hospital, who supervised the arrivals and organized the transportation of the wounded and dead immediately behind the frontlines at the Maslenik front, claimed after glancing at the picture that such a person had never passed through their station. Even if we could have relied on the young woman's memory for faces, which she boasted was excellent, this information didn't amount to much either. Though nobody was ready to openly admit it, it was clear that many of the dead in these battles were buried as late as several days after their death, after the Croatian forces were pushed out. Even then, they were buried at great risk and in haste, without much concern for accurate identification.

These contradictions and the lack of reliable information did not discourage Bulika. She followed even the most unreliable news, any hint of a resolution until the possibility of a further explanation was exhausted.

She left no stones unturned. She spoke to everyone, she went everywhere: The state council of the Red Cross of RSK, the hotel where the representatives of UNPROFOR's civil police had stayed, the headquarters of the Kenyan peacekeeping forces, "Black Chetniks" as they called them for their Serb sympathies; she talked to the volunteers of the Kosmet-Toplice detachment, to "Wolves", Arkan's "Tigers" and the whole Chetnik detachment of SRS; she visited the "Obrovac" pub in Obrovac and the convenience store "Bukovičanka" where the soldiers gathered, sought out peasant refugees from the villages around Maslenica and Peruča ... Wherever there were any hints, Bulika tirelessly followed them in the hope that they led to Bogdan's grave.

In her search, she feared nothing: obsessed, frantic, bewildered, she raced from one place to another, from one alleged witness to another. She ventured closer to the lines of the enemy than soldiers themselves, chased by snipers, grenades literally flying over her head – Croatian ones from Maruna, Jasenice, Rovanjska, Serbian ones from the hill above Zrmanja towards Mala Bobija, Maslenica, Rovanjska. And the grenades seemed to fall literally everywhere and anywhere – into the very centre of town, on to the pub "Obrovac", on to a kiosk when Bulika happened to be only about thirty feet away, another time so physically close to her that it's a true miracle she emerged unwounded.

Still, she couldn't find the true roadsign to Bogdan's grave. And the instant I began discerning traces of fatigue in Bulika's determination, providence intervened for the third time.

When we first arrived in Knin, our guide Slavko mentioned that a certain peasant named Vidosav was in town, looking for his son's grave in the surrounding battlefields. His son's body had disappeared in a pile of cadavers there wasn't any time to bury in the midst of a raging battle. For a long time, Vidosav was hopeful that he would find it and transport it home. Searching, interviewing soldiers, locals and everyone who could in any way help him in his search, he became the true and only expert on graves and battlefields in the bloody circle between Knin, Obrovac, Benkovac, in the hinterland of Novigrad, Pridraga and Pasljuv, on the Maslenik bridge and in Zemunik, between Peruča and Vrlika, on the road to Vodice and Skradine, around Velika Glava and the village of Pamučari and Vujići. Those who wanted to find their sons, husbands and brothers sought the help of Vidosav, already a legend in the local folklore, a sort of sorcerer/ seeker, the eternal father roaming battlefields, a Serbian Wandering Jew who voluntarily remained in the bloody circle, generously helping others find the bodies of their kin since he had no luck in finding his own.

We, however, didn't quite believe Vidosav. Despite Slavko's recommendation, he seemed creepy to us. He reminded us of those miracle-working herbalists trusted by the bearded old peasant women in provincial backwaters.

I remember Bulika telling me when we parted with Vidosav: "Yeah, right. And the newest cure for cancer is – cow's piss!"

Nonetheless, we did tell him everything that could be useful to him in finding the grave. We gave him Bogdan's picture and some basic information, but decided to rely upon the official bodies and participants in the January 27th battles.

We had forgotten about Vidosav. But one day, when Bulika was all but discouraged and ready to give up the search, he turned up at our hotel and said:

"I found the grave."

He had indeed.

A mass grave, in a ditch between the Serbian hamlets Lakatac and Konjane.

Vidosav, the wizard and seeker of lost cadavers.

We reached the hamlets by horse carriage, which Vidosav had rented somewhere for fifty German Marks. When we got to a hill he gave us a signal to stop.

"It's down there. See the ridge?"

We did see it. It could only be reached by foot. We unloaded the coffin, opened it and placed the shovel, spade and quilt (Vidosav had thought of everything) inside. We lifted the coffin and barely wiggling our feet from the mixture of snow and sand, we trudged towards the grave.

"Here it is," Vidosav said.

What lay before us was not a grave of any sort, but a natural indentation in the land where bodies had been lined up and covered with dirt. With deliberately slow motions and in the same, unchanging rhythm, Vidosav began digging up the layers of dirt and throwing them into the distance with broad strokes. Bulika and I stood frozen, our gazes fixed upon the dirt emerging underneath the shovel.

With the third layer of dirt, bodies began to emerge. A shirt sleeve, a naked foot white as bone, a pair of torn lips and teeth full of sand and gravel, a shattered shoulder, a collarbone piercing through the tattered shirt.

Bulika reached for the spade and proceeded to dig away herself. In an instant she stopped, noticing a thick mass of black hair full of grey dirt appearing underneath Vidosav's shovel.

I don't know what was passing through Bulika's head at that moment, but I suddenly realized that in some strange way and for days now, I had been carrying in my mind the very image which now stood before my eyes: Vidosav gouging through a hole full of mutilated bodies white as snow, their faces eaten away, in uniforms soaked with blood connecting body and clothing into large desiccated scabs, bodies mixed with dirt to the point of unrecognizability; a disordered death chamber, messy as a rubbish dump crowned by one glistening, black-haired head.

Bulika squeaked softly, and quickly said in a whisper (worried, I suppose, that Vidosav might hurt Bogdan's face with his shovel):

"Hold it!"

And then, as if the explanation were necessary, she added:

"That's Bonehead."

Vidosav stopped digging and looked at Bulika inquisitively, knowingly, evaluating if she needed help or not. When he saw that she still firmly stood on her two feet, he put away his shovel and began clearing the dirt off Bogdan with his hands.

No face. A smudge. A hole filled with dried blood, brains and mud. A black mane atop the desiccated mass. It struck me that I had once before seen such a thing: I remembered the dog our car ran over on the way to Kragujevac. I remembered a pile of scrambled bloody flesh and quivering fur.

Everything about Bogdan was dead. The skinny uniformed body had shrunk, becoming hardly discernible from the soil covering and shielding it. It seemed whole. Knitted socks on his feet. One of his hands was still in the ground while the other rested on his chest, as if in oath.

Bulika knelt beside the body. She picked up the frozen, muddy hand and kissed it. She shook off the dirt from Bogdan's hair, her relaxed fingers beating through it like the teeth of a brush. She then bent down and kissed the dark-haired head, several times in a row.

She looked like a Muslim in prayer.

She didn't rise from her knees.

She didn't cry.

Vidosav let her kneel. As needed – he had no doubt done it many times before – though no longer than was necessary:

"Come, missus, come," he finally said.

Without a word, he grabbed Bogdan by the shoulders and signalled me to lift his feet. We placed the body on the blanket. Bulika approached and covered Bogdan with the sides of the blanket. She reminded me of a mother, covering her child at night, concerned that he may catch cold.

We placed the body in the coffin. Vidosav let us stand by it while he filled up the hole.

We stood in silence.

We stood for a long time.

Who knows what we thought about.

When he finished, Vidosav put away the shovel and stood by the ditch he had just filled. He crossed himself and as if the cadavers were alive, he spoke to them. His voice was confident at the beginning but grew more and more tremulous:

"Forgive us, my dear sons, for disturbing you in your eternal rest, this Jelena Panić, a student from Belgrade, and I, Vidosav Prokic, a peasant from the foot of the Avala. Alas, you will not profit from this intrusion, but your friend Bogdan will be taken home. God willing, my dear young men, you will also be found by your people, one day. One day, when this fucking war is over, they will find you and take you to your native soil. If I could, my beautiful sons, I would take you all to your homes, I would carry you all, one by one, on my back if I could, if only I knew where you were from, so young and so dead. But I don't know . . . " he said, and began sobbing.

We watched him for a while, and then Bulika did as Vidosav had taught her a moment ago:

"Come, Vidosav, come, old friend," she said.

We couldn't find a car to transport Bogdan's remains. We were relieved when the private carrier "Janicijevic – Trans", agreed to place the coffin on the roof of their bus, providing we covered it with a tarpaulin so as not to terrify the passengers.

We departed from Knin as soon as it got dark, around eight o'clock. The sound of automatic fire from the direction of Novigrad was gradually growing quieter. We were getting further and further away from the pandemonium. Nobody in the bus talked, although many were awake. They stared through their windows at the opaque darkness of the night. An insufferable child was crying monotonously.

Bulika was calm and focused – something rather unusual for her. Following the frantic activity, the tenseness, the obsessive searching, she now sat emptied. She had done her job, probably realizing that she had in fact done nothing. Perhaps I'm wrong. Perhaps she feels better now that she has finally kissed her sweetheart.

I tried finding out:

"How do you feel?" I asked.

I couldn't see her face in the dark.

"Unforgettable," she said.

She said that flatly, with no exclamation mark. Spectrally.

When I heard that dark half-joke, I felt scared for Bulika for the first time. I don't exactly know why. I couldn't see the danger clearly, but I saw it hovering over my friend. I realized, however, that I shouldn't be asking anything in that hour. Better to let her sleep on it.

I tried falling asleep myself, only half-succeeding.

The bus stopped at some checkpoint or other. Drowsy as I was, I couldn't tell where we were. A bearded man dressed in fatigues and carrying a heavy Browning in his hand, climbed in. He stopped at the door and asked:

"Any Muslims?"

Nobody answered.

"I won't touch 'em," he continued, "Just so we know."

The child was still screaming monotonously, annoyingly.

At sunrise, around 7 a.m., two grenades fell, one after the other, to the right and to the left of the road, but far enough from our bus.

"Excuse me, can you tell me where we are?" I asked the driver, who alternated driving shifts with his son.

"On the Majevicki highway," he said, "somewhere between Brusnica and Lukavica. Plenty of shooting around here."

The names of the villages sounded familiar. I realized that they had been mentioned in the erroneous details we had been given by the Information Centre of the East Bosnian Corpus in Bijeljina. I looked at Bulika. I thought she was sleeping. Her head rested against the seat, eyes closed.

"That's where Bonehead was not killed," she said.

Again, there was something about the way she said those words that made me fear for her.

I asked, as one might ask a sick person:

"How do you feel?"

Her eyes remained closed:

"Like shit."

Bogdan Bilogorac was buried on the 17th February in the family grave of the Arandjelović family, at the New Cemetery.

Birdy and Goca invited Bulika to stay with them for a few days. She refused. In the following days, she also turned down my invitations to have lunch together, go to the movies, have a drink at Birdy's. Admittedly, the suggestions were fatuous, but I couldn't think of better ones.

I tried persuading her to finish the book.

"You really ought to do chapter 12. The book really only ends with Bogdan's death."

"Fuck the book. Do whatever you want with it."

She called me on the 28th February, in the middle of the night:

"I sold my place."

"So where are you going to live now?" I asked.

"With Scumbag. I'm going to New Zealand."

"For how long?"

"For ever."

This is how *Premeditated Murder* ends.

With murders and passings on.

This, dear reader, is my epitaph for the dead and the extinct.